The Dramatist

ALSO BY KEN BRUEN

Funeral
Shades of Grace
Martyrs
Rilke on Black
The Hackman Blues
Her Last Call to Louis MacNeice
A White Arrest
Taming the Alien
The McDead
London Boulevard
The Guards
The Killing of the Tinkers
Blitz
The Magdalen Martyrs
Vixen

Ken Bruen

The Dramatist

ST MARTIN'S MINOTAUR NEW YORK

www.minotaurbooks.com

ISBN 0-312-31647-X
EAN 978-0-312-31647-1

First published in Ireland by Brandon, an imprint of Mount Eagle Publications

First U.S. Edition: March 2006

10 9 8 7 6 5 4 3 2 1

For Gabrielle Lord (Queen of Crime) and
Donna Moore (writer par excellence)

The Dramatist

Lemsip and Greek yoghurt. That was my daily fare, the Lemsip for a flu I thought I had. Intermittent sniffles were more likely a throwback to the amount of coke I'd done, but I wasn't admitting that. The yoghurt because I'd read it was good for you—at least I think I had—all those live cultures destroying bacteria. Add a spoon of honey and it's not half bad. Truth was my stomach was a mess and the bios eased it a bit.

For six months I'd been clean and sober. Though if sobriety is related to sanity, I didn't qualify. Not a drop of alcohol had crossed my lips in that time. I hadn't quit coke from any desire to clean up. My dealer got busted and I wasn't able to find another source. I felt so bad without the booze, I figured to kick the coke, too. You're on a roll, go for it. The deadly trilogy, booze, coke and nicotine: the years I'd wasted with them. I was still smoking though. I mean, gimme a break, wasn't I doing pretty damn good? Give or take another block of time, who knew, I'd maybe stop the cigs, too. But the weirdest thing, the down-in-the-crazy-pool most amazing thing . . . I'd begun going to mass.

Phew-oh.

Figure that. One Sunday, gasping for a drink, sick of my own company, I'd walked into the cathedral. Sonny Malloy was singing and, wow, that was a blast. So I went again. It had got to the stage where the priest now nodded, said,

"See you next week."

I liked to sit at the back, watch the sun come creeping through the stained glass windows. As the light spread across the ceiling, I felt something close to peace. The church was always crowded, and the priests were on a time share. So few vocations that they worked on a rota among the parishes. Drink, of course, seemed to attend every level of my life. As I watched the kaleidoscope of colour, I'd re-membered one of the craftsmen who'd worked on those windows. A Dublin guy named Ray, he'd died from cir-rhosis of the liver. His last days, I'd gone to visit him and he said,

"Jack, I'd rather be dead than teetotal."

Got his wish.

Stewart, my drug dealer, had lived by the canal. In ap-pearance he resembled a banker more than a drug dealer. Course, his credo was money. We had an odd relationship: he'd explain the latest product, its effect, its side effects and even the dangers. I seemed to amuse him. How many ex-policemen in their fifties did he supply? I was, in a way, a sort of coup for him. I found him always fascinating. He could only have been in his late twenties and was always impeccably dressed. The personification of the new Irish youth, displaying all the traits of this bright new age: smart, confident, literate, hip, mercenary. They bought into none of the shit we had been reared to. The 1916 Rising meant as much to them as the GAA; in other words, nothing.

I'd been introduced to him by Cathy Bellingham, an ex-punk, ex-junkie from London who'd washed up in Galway. She hooked up with my friend Jeff, a bar owner, and they now had a baby, a Down's syndrome child. When I'd been hurting, and hurting bad, I'd leaned on our friendship to get the name of a dealer. I'd scored from him many times after. Then he got busted and was doing six years in Mountjoy.

I was living in Bailey's Hotel, run by a woman in her eighties. I'd recently been given a new room, almost a self-contained apartment. The feature I liked most was the skylight, for the glimpse of the sky. Man, I felt the endless longing that entails. If I could ever figure out what it was I'd longed for, I might be happy. Didn't seem to be about to happen any time soon. A large wardrobe contained my charity shop clothes. Till recently, I'd owned a leather coat, bought in Camden Lock. It got nicked at mass. If I see a priest wearing it, I will truly throw my hat in. Lined against the wall were my books—a hotchpotch of crime, poetry, philosophy and miscellaneous. They gave me comfort. Some days, they even acted like reassurance.

I was rationing my cigarettes, five a day, and if there's a more subtle torture, I don't know it. As a further step towards shaky rehabilitation, I'd even changed brands. Was now buying Silk Cut, the shittiest level of tar. The ultimate con by the tobacco companies; these Ultra cigs had recently been revealed to be more dangerous than the regular lung busters. I knew this, but my chest seemed to appreciate the gesture. Jeff, my friend, had bought me a month's supply of patches. They sat in a drawer, a mix of recrimination and aspiration. Much like the now depleted clergy.

When Stewart was sentenced, I'd figured that was goodbye. He wasn't the type to do well in prison; they'd eat him alive. The day he was sent down, I was in Nestor's, a tepid coffee before me. I told Jeff about him, laid out the jagged brief history of my dealings with the guy. Jeff, polishing a glass, listened till I was done, asked,

"You're clean now?"

"Off the dope, you mean?"

"Yeah."

"I am."

He put the glass beside a line of gleaming others, said,

"Then fuck him."

I thought that was a little harsh, said,

"That's a little harsh."

Jeff looked me full in the face, took his time, said,

"He was pedalling dope; that's the scum of the earth."

"I kind of liked him."

"That's you all over, Jack, always the odd man out."

Is there a defence to this? I didn't have it. Down the bar sat the perennial sentry. A mainstay of Irish pubs, leastways the old ones, they prop up the counter, a pint glass before them. Always half full—or half empty, depending on your perspective. They rarely talk, save in pronouncements like "We'll never get a summer" or "We won't find it till Christmas."

The World Cup, shambles that it was, had recently finished. Conspiracy theories, dodgy linesmen, atrocious referees had provided a feast of horrendous sport. The sentry said,

"Them Cameroons was robbed."

I stared at him and he added,

"I had a bet on Italy, got 7/1 . . . five goals disallowed. It was a thundering disgrace."

Thing is, he was right. But he became highly suspicious if you ever agreed with him, so I gave a noncommital smile. This seemed to satisfy as he resumed staring into his pint. I don't know what he hoped to find, maybe the lottery numbers or an answer for Eamon Dunphy. I asked Jeff,

"What do I owe you for the coffee?"

"Nada, buddy."

"How's Serena May?"

"She's trying to walk, can't be long now."

"Watch out then, eh?"

Outside Nestor's, I turned up the collar of my garda all-weather coat. A light drizzle was coming down, nothing major. A bunch of South Koreans passed, still dazed from the World Cup. I knew who they were as they'd jackets with "Seoul Rules" on the back. A *double entendre* if ever there was one; ask the Italians.

A former neighbour from my Hidden Valley days was sitting on a bench near the Great Southern Hotel. He hailed me and I walked over. He launched,

"You know I'm no singer. Well, I was in McSwiggan's the other night, I had more than my quota. A Norwegian woman started chatting to me. I knew she was from there, one of them cold countries, she'd a frosty face. All of a sudden I began to sing 'For the Good Times'."

He paused, shaking his head at the wonder of it. I knew Willie Nelson had recently played in Kilkenny, telling a delighted crowd he needed the money to pay the light bill. Now my friend continued,

"She thought the song was gifted, so I told her I wrote it. Jesus, she believed me, and I got to bang her down near the Boat Club. That sort of thing has never happened to me in all my years. I'm thinking I should have taken up singing years ago. What do you make of that?"

"You can't beat Willy."

I left him pondering the mysteries of music and women. It felt good to be walking, and as I passed various pubs, I kept my eyes focused away. The lure of drink lay in wait at every hour of the day. Going over the Salmon Weir

Bridge, I recognised a guy beside the Age Concern bin. He shouted,

"Yo, Jack!"

I'd known him all my life. At school he'd excelled in catechism and was equally fluent in Irish and English. He'd become a poacher or, as they were known locally, snatcher. I said,

"How's it going, Mick?"

He gave a rueful smile, pointed to the water. A man, kitted out in expensive angling gear, with waders to his thighs, was casting a long line. Mick said,

"German bollix."

"Yeah?"

"To fish for one day costs a bloody small ransom, plus handing over half the catch."

A thought struck me and I asked,

"What happens if he only catches one?"

Mick gave a laugh of pure maliciousness, said,

"Then he's fucked."

Mick was probably the finest salmon snatcher west of the Shannon. There was a holdall at his feet, and he leaned down, took out a flask and a full French roll, extended them, asked,

"Want a bite?"

"No, I'm good."

"Have a drink then. It'll warm you up, get the blood dancing."

I felt my heart accelerate, asked,

"What's in it?"

"Chicken soup and poteen."

Christ, I was tempted; just go for it. I shook my head, said,

"No, but thanks."

He put the flask to his head, drank deep; then he lowered it, and I swear his eyes rolled back as he exclaimed,

"Fucking hell."

I envied him the hit. What can compare to that shock of warmth as it hits your stomach? He said,

"I heard you were off it."

I nodded miserably, and he reached again to the bag and asked,

"Want one of these?"

Handed me a calendar with the Sacred Heart on the front, said,

"It's a half-yearly job, so you don't lose six months."

I'd already lost half my life. Flicked it open and there was a homily for each day. I traced my finger down, found that day's date, read,

"True faith promotes justice."

Not in my experience.

I started to hand it back and he refused, going,

"No . . . it's my gift. I mean, you're a mass-goer now, am I right? So this is perfect."

I had an urge to punch him in the mouth. Galway was a city now, a multi-cultural, multi-racial one, but at its core

was the small town mentality. They still knew what you
were at. I shoved the calendar in my pocket, said,

"Be seeing you, Mick."

He waited till I'd gone a distance then chanced,

"Say one for us, will ya?"

I noticed a young man with blond hair across the road;
he seemed to be staring at me. I passed it off.

"When I was writing The Shadow of the Glen *some years ago, I got more aid than any learning could have given me from a chink in the floor of the old Wicklow house where I was staying, that let me hear what was being said by the servant girls in the kitchen."*

J.M. Synge, Preface to
The Playboy of the Western World

I have no family, not in the real sense. My mother and I had been at war for years. A down-in-the-gutter, full-guns-blazing campaign till she had a stroke. To my amazement, I began to ease up on her. She was recovering slowly, and though we'd hardly become close, there had been a definite shift in perspective. I was due to visit her soon. Her minder-companion, Fr Malachy, was as firm as ever in his hatred of me.

Like I gave a shit.

When Jeff and Cathy had their baby, I felt the barrenness of my life was neon-lit. As godfather to the child, I tried to show more interest than I'd have imagined.

Back at Bailey's, I hung the calendar on my wall. Janet, the chambermaid, would be heartened to see it. Time ago, when my drinking was way on the edge, she'd left me a leaflet about Matt Talbot. No doubt my current state she'd attribute to a miracle from Matt. I was definitely on the up.

Had a minifridge in my room, stocked with yoghurt and Galway spring water. Opened a bottle now and stretched on the bed. Flicked the remote and caught the opening of *Oz,* the muscular Australian prison drama. Little did I know the serendipity at work here. If I'd known, would I have acted differently? Right then, my life was on track, as close to normal as it had ever been. Would I have opted to continue the road to citizenship or was I already straining at the leash?

Things were heating up on *Oz.* There'd been an execution, an inmate was dying from AIDS and another was ordered to kill a new arrival. To say it was heavy would be some understatement. I turned it off, then vaguely considered *Six Feet Under,* the HBO series about a family of undertakers. In the last episode, a corpse lost a foot and various mayhem followed involving a gay cop. Thomas Lynch should have sued. I decided to read instead; I'd enough black humour on the streets every day.

Had been dipping into the journals of Jean Rhys. Her sense of displacement always resonated. I'd once heard her described as a citizen of the dispossessed, following a trail of disaster across the dismal landscape of her mind. For a time, she'd lived above a pub in Maidstone . . . during the 1940s, a grim era. She wrote:

"I must write. If I stop writing my life will have been an abject failure. It is that already to other people. But it could be an abject failure to myself. I will not have earned death."

This set off all sorts of bombs in my mind. The phone rang and I put the book aside with relief, went,

"Yeah?"

"Jack, it's Cathy."

"Hi, Cathy."

Pause. I could almost hear her measure her words. Instinct shouted it was going to be heavy, then,

"I need a favour, Jack."

"Sure, hon, if I can."

"Stewart wants you to visit."

"Who?"

A sigh, underlit by impatience.

"The drug dealer . . . *your* drug dealer."

"Oh."

She rushed now: get it out, get it down.

"He's put you on the visitors' list for Wednesday at 3 p.m.; you have to be on time or else it's wait another week."

My mind was running the numbers, but not very well, so I tried to stall.

"But he's in Mountjoy, that's Dublin."

Her patience was gone.

"Unless they moved it."

This was more like her old spark. The Cathy of the punk days, the ex-junkie I'd first met, with barbed wire in her mouth, tattoos along her arms. Truth is, I missed the old version. Since Jeff and the baby, she'd lost her edge, had mutated into a gombeen pseudo-Irish colleen.

Jesus.

Now she waited. I faltered, said,

"Cathy, I don't know about this."

She'd been expecting such, said,

"He'll pay your expenses, booked you a room in the Royal Dublin. Wouldn't want you inconvenienced at any stage, would we, Jack? Think of it as a holiday."

I didn't answer and she said,

"You owe, Jack."

"Hey, Cathy, give me a break. I paid him for his services . . . he was a frigging drug dealer. How do I owe him?"

"Not him; you owe me."

This was true. I tried to find some words to get off the hook but none came. I said,

"You've got me, I guess."

If she was relieved, she wasn't letting it show, said,

"I've left an envelope with Mrs Bailey. It's got cash, train times and the hotel reservation."

"You were pretty certain I'd agree."

"Well, even you, Jack, have a sense of obligation."

I felt this was a cheap shot. For Chrissakes, I was godfather to her child. I countered with,

"You seem to have covered all the angles."

Heard her intake of breath, then,

"If I'd all the angles covered, Jack, I'd have ended my friendship with you a long time ago."

And she hung up.

During my years as a guard, I'd met all kinds of people, usually the scum of the earth. A time I was stationed in Cavan, I arrested an old man for urinating in a public place. Yeah, Cavan was high crime zone. Got him in the car and I did feel petty. He said,

"Son, the thing with friends is they aren't ever, and I mean ever, allowed to make you feel bad. That's the role of the rest of the world."

I was young then, full of piss and wind, said in my Templemore tone,

"I'm not your friend."

He gave a tired smile, said,

"Sure, guards have no friends."

I forget his face but I remember his words. Was I angry with Cathy? Let me put it this way, I was going to have a hard job explaining to Mrs Bailey why I punched a hole in the bathroom wall. Didn't break my knuckles but it was a close call.

Mrs Bailey handed me a fat envelope, said,

"That young girl, Cathy? . . . She left it for you."

"Thanks."

I hefted the envelope in my palm, figuring this was a lot of cash. Mrs Bailey was staring at me and I snapped,

"What?"

Probably a little sharper than I intended. She took a step back, then,

"That girl Cathy . . . she's not one of our own, not Irish I mean?"

"No, she's from London."

"She has a breed of an Irish accent."

"Yes, she went native."

She clucked her tongue, shook her head, dismissing such nonsense, said,

"They think if they buy a Claddagh ring and use the

Lord's name, it makes them one of us, as if that could ever happen."

I gave a tight smile, turned to go, said,

"Sorry if I was a bit sharp."

She assessed me, then,

"You were sharp, and I don't think you're sorry. I think you regret the action as you're fond of that control. 'Tis the guard in you."

I didn't think there was a whole lot to be gained in debating the point so I said,

"I'll be in Dublin for two days."

"Oh, are you working again?"

"No, it's to visit someone."

"Are they sick?"

"As a parrot."

I'd a holdall on my shoulder, wasn't entirely sure what to pack for prison. Put in two white shirts; they'd cover most contingencies. A pair of Farah slacks with that knife crease, you could slice bread with it. Two books, of course, to cover both legs of the trip. I'd been into Charlie Byrne's on Monday. A ton of new books had arrived, and I wished I had the time to go through them. Vinny was engrossed in a book, then he looked up, the slow grin beginning, said,

"Jack, we thought you'd given up reading."

"Never happen."

"Help you with anything?"

I glanced round, no one near, and asked,

"I'm going to see a guy in prison; I thought I'd bring him some books. Any ideas?"

He shifted his glasses, a sure indication of serious consideration, said,

"I'd stay away from prison accounts. I mean, the guy is

doing time. How much is he going to want to read about it?"

As if he read my mind. God forgive me, I'd been seriously contemplating exactly that line of country. He reached behind him, to what I knew to be his private stash, pulled out one.

"Here."

Spike Milligan's *Puckoon*. I said,

"This is your own copy: looks well handled and well cared for."

"Jack, what's the worst that can happen, they'll nick it? They're already serving the sentence."

"How much do I owe you?"

"I'll put it on your account."

"Thanks, Vinny, you'll be rewarded."

"From your lips to God's ears."

The train was due to leave Tuesday at 11 a.m. I'd plenty of time to kill, walked up to the cathedral and was relieved not to meet the snatcher. On by the hospital, on towards Cooke's Corner. The rain started and I turned my collar up. As I turned into Mill Street I decided to buy cigarettes. For as long as I remember, there's been a family grocery there. I noted it was now a mini-mart and wondered how much time had gone since my last visit. Walked in and got my second surprise: it was mini Africa. Black families chatted in the aisles, their kids spread out along the wall. Energetic music spilled from every corner. A jovial large man clapped my shoulder, said,

"Welcome, man."

I moved to the till and a woman in her thirties with a face of stunning beauty served me. As I turned to leave, she said,

"Please visit soon."

"I will."

The rain had stopped and I passed by the garda station . . . or the barracks as it used to be known. It was a hive of activity. I paused for a moment, a jumble of emotions. Did I miss being a guard? Oh God, yes. Did I miss the bullshit? Never. I wondered how it would go if I called in to see my old nemesis, Clancy. Was I kidding? I knew exactly how that would go.

Badly.

A man in his fifties, with red protruding cheeks, purple nose, tweed jacket and the regulation blue shirt did a double take, asked,

"Jack?"

"Hello, Brian."

If memory served, as it sometimes did, we'd pulled crowd duty in the days of cattle boats. Right down to his GAA tie and the gold *fáinne,* he was beyond caricature. No faking the gruff friendliness though as he bellowed,

"By the holy, I heard you were dead."

"Close enough."

He looked round and I knew it didn't help any career to be seen with me. He offered,

"Have you time for a quick one?"

"I have a train to catch."

"You are convicts. Your job here is to lie, cheat, steal, extort, get tattoos, take drugs, sell drugs, shank and sock each other. Just don't let us catch you—that's our job. We catch you, you got nothing coming."

Jimmy Lerner, *You've Got Nothing Coming: Notes from a Prison Fish*

I couldn't remember the last time I caught the train; and what the hell had happened to the station? Of course, I knew that coach travel, rail strikes and price hikes had played havoc with the service, but the station was transformed totally. Before, it had been a country train station servicing what was, in reality, a country town. The station master knew everybody in Galway, and not only did he know where you were going but the purpose of the trip. No matter the number of years you might have been gone, when you alighted at the station he'd greet you by name and know where you'd been.

A speaker announced departures in four languages. I queued for my ticket behind a line of backpackers. Not a word of English anywhere. Finally I got to order a two-day return and was staggered at the price, asked,

"Is that first class?"

"Don't be silly."

Muttering, I passed the new modern restaurant, the old draughty café but a blip in the mind. There'd been a photo of Alcock and Brown pinned to the wall beside a poster of a jolly man staring in wonder at a flock of flamingos, pints of the black in their beaks, and the logo

> My Goodness
> My Guinness.

It always brought a smile.

The train still retained a smoking carriage, to the astonishment of an American couple. She went,

"John, you can, like . . . smoke . . . on this train."

If he had an answer, he wasn't voicing it. I had the carriage to myself. So I lit up, feeling it was downright mandatory. A whistle blew and we pulled away. Louis MacNeice loved trains and always wrote his journal during trips. I tried to read to no avail. Outside Athlone, a tea trolley came, pushed by a powerfully built man. He looked as if he moved mountains. The trolley appeared a mere irritant. I asked,

"How you doing?"

"Tea, coffee, cheese sandwich, chocolate, soft drinks?"

His accent was thick, near impenetrable. I was able to deduce the list of goodies from a list attached to the side of the trolley. I pointed to the tea, and as he poured and placed it before me, the movement of the train caused half of it to spill. He put a thick finger to his chest, said,

"Ukraine."

I could have thumped my chest, gone,

"Irish."

But felt a level of alcohol was necessary for that. I gave him ten euro and he grabbed it, moved on. For less than a quarter plastic cup of coloured water, he was on a winner. I took an experimental taste and it was as bad as I've ever had—a blend of bitterness that hints at tea and coffee and brought to a fine art by Iarnród Éireann.

I heard the carriage door slide open behind me, then a woman's voice:

"Jack? Jack Taylor?"

Turned to see a woman in her late twenties, dressed in what used to be called a twin set. Now they'd call it bad taste. The sort of outfit you saw on British television drama, usually involving a bridge game and a body in the library. Her face could have reached prettiness if she'd made the slightest effort. Tiny pearl earrings gave me the clue I needed. I said,

"Ridge . . . give me a moment, Bridie . . . no . . . Bríd?"

She gave a gasp of annoyance.

"We don't use the English form. I told you that like . . . so many times . . . it's Nic an Iomaire."

The ban garda. We hadn't so much collaborated as collided on a previous case. I'd eventually helped her gain credit on a major crime, though my help was highly suspect and definitely tainted. Our connection was fraught from the beginning. Her uncle, Brendan Flood, and I had

had a mixed history, beginning as adversaries and ending as uneasy friends. His research and information had been vital to most of my work; then he became a born-again and his zeal had danced along my nerves. Then came his breakdown, through drink, loss of family and the abandonment of all belief. I'd spent a booze-lit session with him where we'd drank boilermakers and mainlined nicotine. I failed to pick up on the level of his despair. A few days later, he'd taken a solid kitchen chair, a rope, and hanged himself.

To add to my guilt, he'd bequeathed me a chunk of money and the ban garda. Her, I tried to lose at every turn. Here she was again. She sat awkwardly into the opposite seat and I offered,

"Get you something?"

I indicated my plastic cup, added,

"I can recommend the tea and it isn't cheap."

I never actually believed people turned up their noses but she achieved it—looked like she'd a lot of practice—said,

"I don't drink tea."

"Jeez, what a surprise. If memory serves, our times in the pub, you had orange juice and, wow, that memorable time, you kicked against the traces, had a wine spritzer."

"But, of course, Mr Taylor, you drank enough for all of us."

Here was the old feeling, the urge to slap her in the mouth, settled for,

"I'm off the booze."

"Oh . . . and how long will that last . . . this time?"

I sat back, reached for my cigs, and she near spat,

"I'd really prefer if you didn't do that."

I lit up, said,

"Like that would ever be a consideration."

She waved her hand in front of her face, the universal flag of serious irritation by non-smokers. I asked,

"You going to Dublin?"

"Yes, court observation. The super has decreed all ranks must attend the Four Courts, see how justice is dispensed."

I could see the bureaucrats coming up with this brainwave, said,

"Let me save you the trip: it's dispensed badly. With the shortage of uniforms on the street, it's vital the guards get observation experience. So did you get promotion?"

A cloud passed her face, touched the corners of her eyes. She said,

"Oh yeah, right, like they're going to upgrade someone of my orientation."

I was confused, said,

"Because you're a woman?"

She was out of patience, went,

"What, you don't know?"

What the hell was she on about? I truly had lost the thread, asked,

"Know what?"

"That I'm gay."

God knows, for a so-called investigator, I am blind in all

the obvious areas. There have been times, albeit rare, when I've made impressive deductive leaps. For the rest, it seemed like life sailed on by with me in the constant dark. There are probably a million permutations on the correct reply to the admission "I'm gay". Apart from noises of solidarity, empathy, support, there are even replies that include not only encouragement but humour. I came up with,

"Oh."

She stared at me and I grasped the meaning of "a loaded silence". That's what we had for the next five minutes. Then she stood, said,

"I must return to my seat. Margaret will be wondering where I am."

Was Margaret the significant other? I hadn't the balls to ask. She looked at the rack above me, no luggage, said,

"You're up for the day."

I wanted rid of her, said,

"I'm going to jail."

"It's where you belong."

And was gone.

At Heuston I lingered on the platform, hoping for a glimpse of her—well, of Margaret really—but they'd given me the slip. I hopped on a bus and it went straight to O'Connell Street.

What a dump.

Jesus, whatever we were doing in Galway, it had to be better than this. The once impressive street was cheap, dirty and depressing.

As I headed for the Royal Dublin, a middle-aged man stopped, whispered,

"Do you know where the Ann Summers sex shop is?"

"What? . . . Are you kidding? How the fuck would I know?"

Thought, steady, you'll have to get a grip.

The hotel had an impressive foyer and the receptionist was friendly, asked,

"Has Sir a reservation?"

I did.

And,

"Does Sir require smoking or non-smoking?"

Take a wild bloody guess.

My visit was slotted for 3 p.m. so I caught a cab, said,

"Mountjoy, please."

The driver eyed me but didn't comment. Silent taxi drivers don't exist and after a few minutes came,

"Is that a Galway accent?"

"Yes."

I said it in a tone to discourage further inquiry. It didn't work.

"Long trip to the Joy for you, eh?"

He took my answering grunt as interest, said,

"You'll have seen the match on Sunday?"

I hadn't but that makes no difference. I didn't even know which one he meant and certainly wasn't about to ask. In Ireland, there is always a match and, more to the point, there is always one to discuss. I tuned him out. Finally, the cab stopped and he said,

"There she is, second home to the cream of the country."

I got out and he asked,

"Want me to wait?"

"No, could be a while."

"That's what they all say."

He burned rubber as he took off. No doubt the sound was bitter music to the carjackers behind the walls. I stared

at the prison for a moment and lit a cig. My daily quota
would be shot to hell. Looking, I felt a dread along my
spine. The very appearance was intimidating, and no way
would you mistake it for anything other than what it was:
a place of deprivation, of punishment. I shook myself and
headed in. Not an easy building to gain access to; the number of checks and double-checks took ages. My time as a
guard wasn't cutting me any slack. Eventually, I took my
position with the other visitors, predominantly women and
young children. They seemed to know each other well and
engaged in a mocking banter. It was almost like bingo
night. Sign of the new Ireland was the two black women.
They sat apart and seemed drained of all emotion, a weariness hanging above them.

Then a warden shouted and the visitors shuffled forward. I was body searched again and the contents of my
plastic bag examined. *Puckoon* was opened, felt, even the
spine was handled, then I was passed through.

"*I am neither an occultist nor a mystic. I am a child of my time despite all forebodings and I hold strictly to what I see. But there is a frightful riddle here, and I come back again and again to what appears to me to be the answer. What I saw gliding by there, like the Prince of Darkness himself, was no human being.*"

Friedrich Reck-Malleczewen,
Diary of a Man in Despair

Put it down to movies. I'd expected our meeting to take place with glass between us, using phones to communicate. I was wrong. The inmates sat at tables, watchful wardens at the wall. A vending machine was in full flow, and the atmosphere was almost like a picnic. Took me a minute to focus. Stewart was in the middle of the room, raised his arm. I moved over, not sure how I should behave. It wasn't like I was family or even a friend. He was wearing a denim shirt, loose jeans—too loose. I'd anticipated him losing weight, but he had the flabbiness you get from starchy food and no exercise. Already he had the prison pallor, and his left eye was bruised, almost closed. I gave him the book and he put out his hand, said,

"Thanks for coming."

I took his hand and we shook. His former appearance of smugness, money and comfort was gone, replaced by a fierce control, as if he was willing his eyes not to dart wildly in all directions. I sat, nodded at his eye, asked,

"What happened?"

He gave a vague smile, not even aware of it, said,

"A minor disagreement, over a rice pudding. It's what prison is about really, who gets to eat your dessert."

I didn't know a whole lot about this and said nothing.

He touched his eye delicately, said,

"I'm learning though; I've hired a minder. I was always a fast study, but it took me a while to adapt."

I was curious, asked,

"How's that work, the minder?"

A small laugh, then,

"Like everything else, on money. I pay the biggest thug to mind my back."

I couldn't picture it, said,

"I thought they'd have frozen your accounts. I mean, isn't that what they do, with drug money?"

Now he gave a full smile and I noticed he still had his teeth. The minder was earning his wages. He said,

"They froze some of the accounts. I was always smart with money, it's no big thing. You get a sharp solicitor, you're in the game."

I looked round at a continuous line for the snacks, the forced smiles on the faces of the visitors and the bored eyes of the wardens. I asked,

"You call this being in the game?"

He let his control slip and I glimpsed a scared kid, but he reined it in, said,

"I had a sister, Sarah."

I noted the tense, echoed,

"Had?"

"Two weeks before my bust, she was found dead."

"I'm sorry."

He tilted his head to the side, as if he was listening to some faraway music, then,

"You didn't know her, why on earth would you be sorry?"

I was going to say "Well, then fuck you," but he continued,

"Sarah Bradley. Twenty years old, final year at NUI, doing an arts degree. Look . . ."

He reached in his shirt, took out a photo, slid it over. A very pretty girl, black curls framing two large eyes, strong cheekbones and wide open smile, brilliant white teeth. The camera had caught a sense of quiet confidence, a girl who knew exactly what she was doing. I said,

"Lovely girl."

And slid it back. He let it lie, said,

"She lived in Newcastle Park, shared a house with two other girls. They were at a party and when they got home, they found her at the foot of the stairs. Her neck was broken."

He stared at me and I said,

"Terrible accident."

"No, it wasn't."

I'd lost the thread, tried,

"You don't think it was terrible?"

"I don't think it was an accident."

That hit me blindside; I began to see where this was going, the purpose of my visit. I reached for my cigs and said,

"Whoa . . ."

He put up his hand, near barked,

"Don't smoke! I have nicotine clouds 24/7, so allow me a little breathing space."

What the hell, I decided to humour him. A drug dealer intolerant of smoke was beyond comment. Not to mention the blitzkrieg of smoking from the other inmates. He used his hands to hold his face, then physically geared his body, continued,

"Under my sister's body, under Sarah's body, was a book by Synge."

"Synge?"

"Even you'll have heard of *The Playboy of the Western World*. Sarah hated him, all that keening bullshit. She wouldn't have him in the house, and before you start, it didn't belong to the other girls. I asked. They never saw it before."

I rallied my thoughts, then,

"Come on, Stewart, you said she was studying an arts course; Synge had to be on it."

He leaned over and I could smell his breath, a mix of toothpaste and breath freshener. His face was intense.

"All I'm asking is you check it out. I'll pay well, very well. Here, I've written her address, details . . . Please, Jack."

I don't know what it takes to get you through prison, what obsession pulls you through the days. I decided to be honest—never a smart move.

"Stewart, I don't think there's anything to check out."

He lay his hands flat on the table, summoned all his energy, said,

"So you've nothing to lose. You get a fat payday for, what . . . a few inquiries? I've never, and I mean never, asked anyone for a single thing. In court, the solicitor suggested, as a first time offender, I ask for consideration. I didn't and here I am, begging you."

I had hoped to never check out another death. I'd become involved with the previous cases against my instincts and with horrendous results.

I decided to go through the motions, asked,

"What did the guards say?"

He gave a short, sharp laugh. Heads turned from other tables and he said,

"Get real, Jack. A dope dealer's going to get a lot of help from them? What they said was, pity it wasn't me broke my bloody neck."

"Was there a coroner's report?"

"Sure. No drugs or alcohol in her system; the verdict was misadventure. What do you think? Should I put that on her headstone?"

People were standing, getting coats, and I felt a wave of relief, said,

"OK, I'll take a look, but I can't promise anything."

He put out his hand, said,

"Thanks, Jack, and thanks for the book: Spike Milligan, perfect material for this madhouse. You won't regret helping me, I guarantee it."

Boy, was he ever wrong about that.

Back in the waiting room, a warden was escorting us out, touched my arm, whispered,

"You're Jack Taylor?"

"Yeah."

"Used to be a guard?"

I was taken aback, considered denying it but went,

"That's right."

"And now you're visiting drug pushers?"

A flash of anger surfaced and I debated telling him to go fuck himself. Alas, I might need to visit again, though I fervently hoped not, said,

"So?"

He moved me along, then,

"No wonder they kicked your ass out. You're a bloody disgrace."

Outside as the gates closed, my face still smarting from the remark, I had a powerful urge to drink. Could taste

Jameson in my mouth, feel my hand reach for a pint of the black, sink the first in a series. I had almost decided to go for it when a taxi passed. I hailed it. As we took off, I didn't look back. The driver said,

"You know why Man U should never have bought Rio Ferdinand?"

I was thinking about a man named Michael Ventris, who deciphered Linear B. Lived his whole life trying to crack the hieroglyphs dating back 4,000 years inscribed on stones unearthed in Crete and for decades posing the greatest puzzle in archaeology and linguistics. Ventris finally solved it, but the achievement left him empty. He ended his life by driving into the back of a lorry. His lifelong obsession had gone; the most extraordinary mind of his decade had lost focus. I was sorely tempted to grab the driver, go,

"Shut the fuck up, here's a story."

Then ask,

"What happens when you get to the top and it's barren, a wilderness?"

We'd arrived in O'Connell Street and he was going,

"Don't even get me started on Leeds."

I paid him and found the urge to drink had abated. Crossed the street to the Kylemore and ordered steak and chips. Ate it without tasting a bite. The waitress said,

"You enjoyed that."

"Yes."

"Dessert? We've some lovely apple tart and custard."

I passed.

How to kill the night in Dublin? Thing was, I felt edgy, off balance. If I'd been drinking, I'd have headed for Mooney's, end of story. Instead I went into the hotel, asked for my room key. The girl gave me a smile, asked,

"Are you enjoying your stay?"

"Immensely."

In the room, I contemplated a bath but couldn't summon the energy. Lay on the bed and figured a nap would revive me. Slept twelve hours. Dreamt of my father. He was holding a book by Synge, said,

"The answers are here."

"But I don't even know the questions."

I think I was shouting. Then I was in a cemetery, trying to read the names on the headstones, but they all said Linear B. I don't recall the rest, but obviously it was distressing, as I woke with tears on my cheeks. I said aloud,

"What the hell was that about?"

Showered and packed up. My plan to do the round of bookshops was no longer appealing, so I caught the train at 11 a.m. No trolley service; I think I missed the Ukrainian. Now I was able to read and had been anticipating *High Life* by Matthew Stokoe. Started it as we hit the outskirts of Dublin and never looked up till we reached Athenry.

It was Chandler on heroin, Hammet on crack, James M. Cain with a blowtorch, and it matched my mood with a wild ferocity. The writing was a knuckleduster to the brain, a chainsaw to the gut. It not so much rocked as walloped the blood with a rush of pure amphetamine. The prose sang and screamed along every page, a cesspit of broken lives illuminated with a taste of dark euphoria. I felt downright feverish. How often is a novel like a literary blow to the system? I felt Jim Thompson would have killed for this. If James Ellroy had indeed abandoned the crime genre, then here was his dark heir.

I closed the book, feeling I'd run a marathon. Not once had I thought of Stewart or his sister. The train was crossing the bridge over Lough Atalia, and as I stared out at the bay, dark clouds hanging on the horizon, I didn't know if I had a sense of homecoming. I think you require a modicum of peace for that. I went into Roches, passed the booze counter real fast and bought some groceries. Decided to leave the Greek yoghurts and Lemsips alone. I was healthy enough. As I paid at the till, I looked up and there was the blond young guy again. He eyed me for a moment and then was gone. Put it down to coincidence.

Mrs Bailey was at reception, said,

"Welcome back."

I reached in my bag, pulled out a packet, handed it over. Her eyes lit, she exclaimed,

"I love presents."

She tore off the paper, went,

"Bewley's fudge, oh my, they give me teethaches."

"Oops."

"Oh no, I'll be delighted to have the ache. Lets you know you're alive."

I left her chewing energetically, surprised she had real

teeth. I went to my room, checked my bookcase and, as I anticipated, not a single volume of Synge.

Looked at the Sacred Heart calendar and the day's entry read:

"Don't be enslaved by wealth."

I'd do my best.

"Working a case is like living a life. You could be going along with your head down, pulling the plow as best you can, but then something happens and the world isn't what you thought it was anymore. Suddenly the way you see everything is different, as if the world has changed color, hiding things that were there before and revealing things you otherwise would not have seen."

Robert Crais, *L.A. Requiem*

Next morning, I was reading an interview with Marc Evans, the director of *My Little Eye,* the classy Brit horror movie. A line he said triggered all types of memories:

"Our cameras aren't showing you where the action is, they're following it."

I sat and thought about that, why it had such an impact. Was it some skewed metaphor for my life or simply a smart perspective? I made some coffee—had moved up to real coffee—yeah, beans, filters, the whole nine yards. What I liked best was the aroma: just let it cook, simmer and allow that smell bounce off the wall. I never ever tired of the sensation. Early mornings, if you get down to Griffin's Bakery, they make a loaf called a grinder. Aw fuck, this is bread to trade your soul for, but the true bliss is that as you approach, the tang of fresh baking permeates the upper part of the street. It's beyond comfort, beyond analysis.

Real coffee comes from the same neighbourhood. Took

me a while to readjust. When you've drunk instant all your life, you are seriously fucked. The real thing is too much; you can't get your taste around it. Plus it packs one hell of a punch: two cups and you're off your feet. All my years of caffeine, it was purely to punctuate the hangovers.

Drank it and chased it with cig number one. This five cigs a day gig was not working, but I'd worry about that later. I dressed in a white shirt, black cords, checked myself in the mirror. Looked like I was selling something and not anything you'd ever need. My eyes were bright, clear. Six months clean and sober and here was the payoff. If only I could pass the message along to my soul.

Took out my notebook, read the few details I had on Sarah Bradley: age twenty, student, final year. She lived— had lived—in Newcastle Park, No. 13. The address had surely been ill-starred. I figured this investigation would take all of ten minutes. The sun was shining and I stood at Eyre Square for a moment. The grass was packed with sunbathers. By evening, they'd be red and blistered, the whole sum of an Irish summer.

As I passed the GBC café, I don't know what prompted me to glance in the window. My heart did a jig. At a table was Ann Henderson, the love of my life. I'd been investigating her daughter's suicide and fell in love. My drinking had driven her away. Was I over her? Was I fuck?

All my instincts roared "Keep moving". I was about to, but the set of her shoulders, the way she was seated, something was wrong. A voice in my head asking,

"And this is your problem how?"

Yeah, right.

After she'd left me, she hooked up with a guard, name of Coffey. He was, in the memorable words of Superintendent Clancy,

"A big thick yoke."

On the grapevine, I heard they'd recently got married. My hope had been they'd move . . . preferably to Albania. I had managed to avoid all word of them since.

I pushed open the door, approached, went,

"Ann."

She jumped. If not out of her skin, close to. Her head came up, and the first thing I noticed was the bruise on her left cheekbone; had seen enough to know there was only one explanation. A fist. Her eyes, way and beyond her best feature, were shadowed, haunted. Took her a minute to focus then,

"Jack . . . Jack Taylor."

Was she glad to see me? No, the look in her eyes was misery unabated. I indicated a chair, asked,

"Can I join you?"

Not a difficult question, but it seemed to throw her, as if she was prepared to bolt. I sat, asked,

"What's wrong?"

A waitress was approaching and Ann burst into tears. The waitress glared at me and I tried to indicate,

"Hey, I just joined the party, don't lay this on me."

I waved her off, and she had the face of someone who's

considering calling the guards. I wanted to reach out, touch Ann, but felt it would freak her further so I waited. Her shoulders convulsed as silent sobs racked her. Finally, they subsided and she reached for tissues, began to dab at her eyes, said,

"I'm sorry."

Why wasn't I one of those guys who'd have produced a brilliant white hankie and helped her dry her tears? I asked,

"For what? You're feeling bad; it's not a crime."

Slight smile then,

"I must look a fright."

To me? . . . never. But kept that to myself. I'd a hundred questions, went with,

"How about some coffee, maybe a slice of Danish? . . . Hey, I know, they do a wicked cheesecake."

She looked at me then. The time, briefly, we'd been lovers, her afterglow was hot chocolate and cheesecake. Me? Just relief to lie beside her, the very beat of my heart. She said,

"Coffee would be good. Will you excuse me while I repair my face?"

Women can do that. Be destroyed with grief, go to the ladies' room and return like a movie star. Guys? Well, they don't do grief well, unless you count a six pack and Sky Sports a consolation. I signalled to the waitress. Grudgingly, she approached and I asked,

"Two coffees?"

She had the face of someone who's going to knife you, growled,

"Cream?"

"Good thinking. Let's shoot the works."

She stomped off. I figured she hadn't read the lines of "Desiderata" recently. I planned on checking what the Sacred Heart calendar had to make of this. Better be good or it was bin time. The coffee came and, recent expert as I was, I could tell it was instant. The smell is the give-away. No wonder the glossy mags have articles on caffeine snobs.

Ann returned, her face remade. Her eyes, though . . . they hadn't yet found a cover for agony, at least not emotionally. Giving a timid smile, she sat and uttered the line which kills conversation dead:

"So, Jack, tell me all your news."

Maybe it's age or I've become cantankerous, but I'm almost all done with chit-chat, the small talk of vacancy. I bluntly went,

"Cut the shit."

Knocked her back but I wasn't done.

"I haven't seen you for ages and you trot out all that polite crap. You have obviously been knocked around and what? . . . We're going to chat about the weather? Give me a bloody break."

Jeez, I hoped the waitress wasn't in earshot. Ann looked ready to bolt, then reached for her cup, took a sip, a tiny tremor in her hand. She took a deep breath, then,

"You know I got married?"

I nodded, misery enveloping my heart. My eyes clocked her finger, a shiny gold ring. She twisted at it absently. Of all the routes your mind travels, especially when it's threatened, I remembered a mad notion my psycho friend Sutton had once laid on me. We'd been to a pub in North Kerry, one of those old establishments where, come three in the morning, the owner plonks the keys on the counter, goes,

"Lock up when you're finished, lads."

Yeah, that kind of rare place, a treasure beyond estimation. I was still in the guards and pulling student duty. This involved hassling college kids, busting pot parties, dragging them out of rivers—a duty that grinds you down. My two-day leave, Sutton and I had gone on a serious drinking jaunt. Serious in that we drank solid, no pit stops. Even through the hangovers and clear on through to the other side. Committed partying. Sutton went behind the bar, began to build two more frothy black pints, left them to mature and grabbed a jar of eggs in liquid from the bottom shelf, said,

"Pickled, by God . . . like us I suppose. Want one?"

I didn't so he ate two, and as he munched he went,

"Jack, did I ever tell you about men who play with their wedding band?"

I'd have remembered, said,

"No."

He tilted his head back, dropped a full egg in his mouth, chewed like a horse, then,

"Guy fiddles with his ring, he's oversexed."

I'd dismissed it with a shrug, but down the years, I see a man toy with the wedding band, I go . . . "Uh oh."

Back to Ann, her question if I knew she got married: did I ever? Said,

"I heard."

She fixed her eyes on a place above my eyes, began,

"Tim, my husband, he's not a bad man, but he gets . . . frustrated."

Thought to myself, "That's what they're calling it now." Kept my voice neutral, asked,

"By what?"

She waved her hand, a gesture of vagueness.

"It's not like when you were in the force, Jack. Being a guard today is almost impossible. After Abbeylara, after that schoolteacher killed his daughter, the public have turned against the police. It makes him so angry . . . he . . . he lashes out. He doesn't mean it."

Here is the greatest excuse in the Irish psyche. No matter what shit goes down, what evil is perpetrated, the song remains the same: "They didn't mean it."

Course they did, and usually with malice aforethought. If you ever reach a level of forgiveness, your prayer can only be:

"Father forgive them though they bloody did know what they did."

I reached for a cig, and now I had a slight tremor.

She said,

"Ah, Jack, them lads will kill you."

Had to bite down, not answer:

"Much like husbands."

Buying time, I took a belt of the caffeine, and yeah, freeze dried. Asked,

"And so he beats you?"

The shame in her face, that awful look of victims, the added horror of crimes when the victim feels they de-served it.

Jesus.

She said,

"There's been awful pressure, accusations of bribery. Tim, he loves being a guard. If he wasn't . . . he'd . . ."

The Tim Coffey I remembered would build a nest in your ear and charge you rent. The type of asshole who was "big in the GAA", the truth being he was just big. Like natural bullies, he'd survive anywhere. I said,

"He'd what? End up like me?"

Her face showed she hadn't meant that. She hadn't, as the Americans say, "connected the dots" or "done the math". I realised with a jolt she probably didn't think about me at all.

She said,

"I'm sorry, Jack, I didn't mean anything. Anyway, I started to nag; it's what women do when they're fright-ened. I tried to stop but it was like the devil was in me. Tim has a temper, and he lost it."

The current buzz expression, excuse abuse. Losing it has replaced vicious fucker in every sense. A guy shoots his family, says, "I lost it."

I was losing it myself, asked,

"Just the once?"

Barbed wire in every nuance.

"Sorry?"

"He walloped you one time, that it?"

"Yes."

She was lying and I could understand that, maybe even sympathise a little. A thought struck her and, alarmed, she went,

"You won't do anything, Jack?"

"Do? What could I possibly do? He's a guard."

Then the worst moment: she grabbed my hand and I felt the electricity. Christ, you build a wall round your feelings, a veritable fortress to insulate your nerve endings, and one lousy touch, the whole defence crumbles. Fuck and fuck again. She was pleading,

"Jack, I need you to promise, give me your word."

I stood up, felt almost dizzy and definitely nauseous. I reached for some money, scattered it on the table, said,

"I can't promise that."

Got outside and the rain was teeming down. When the fuck did that happen? My white shirt was drenched and a passing car sprayed a wave of dirty water over my pants. I could have killed somebody. Turned left, muttered,

"I have an investigation to do. That's what I'll do, I'll investigate."

Passing the Abbey, a fellah I think I knew said,

"Talking to yourself, that's not a good sign."

Tell me about it!

"For evil arises in the refusal to acknowledge our own sins."

Scott Peck, *People of the Lie*

When I got to Newcastle Park, the house where Sarah Bradley had lived, I had to kick-motivate myself. The voice going,

"What a waste of time, not to mention bloody reckless."

I knocked on the door, opened by an extremely ugly girl in dungarees and bare feet. Dirty bare feet.

She snapped,

"What?"

Like that.

I was tempted to say,

"Well, you could wash your feet for a start."

Began my spiel as I fast-flicked my wallet at her. It had an expired driver's licence and my library card.

"Sorry to bother you. I'm from Mutual Alliance, and there is a life policy on your former flatmate, Sarah Bradley. I need to check a few points."

She shouted over her shoulder,

"Peg, there's some guy from the insurance company, are you decent? . . . oh . . . I'm Mary."

I didn't catch the muffled reply, but it didn't sound like welcome. Mary waved me in, moving ahead of me down a hall. The student aroma of curry, feet, beer, trainers and forced bonhomie. Peg wasn't much to look at either, but she wasn't having a problem with it. Dressed in a thigh-slit nightie, she came down the stairs, yawning. Her body language suggested she knew how to utilise that body.

She said in a Beavis/Butthead accent,

"Shit, I need some coffee, like yesterday."

She probably hadn't studied *Clueless* but she'd definitely taken lessons from *Popular.*

I was staring at the foot of the stairs, where Sarah had died.

Peg said,

"Let's park it in the kitchen."

Now she was Susan Sarandon. I followed. The room was like it had been hit by a careless bomb. Clothes, books, CDs, empty Chinese cartons (least I hoped they were empty), tights, bras, wine bottles with stubs of candles and discarded roach papers.

Mary was making coffee, asked,

"Get you some?"

"No, I'm good."

I perched on a hard chair, got my notebook out, said,

"Just a few questions and I'm . . . like gone."

See how Peg liked the echo treatment. It didn't register. She gave me a coy look above the rim of her cup, said,

"You look like a guard."

I gave her my shy smile, as if I was secretly pleased. I wasn't entirely sure how to smile like a guy in insurance, but predatory had to be a good start. I asked,

"Was Sarah clumsy? I mean, would falling down be something she might be likely to do?"

Peg glanced at Mary and I tried to read it but failed. Peg rooted for a cigarette in a pile of crushed boxes, found one, lit it from the cooker, said to Mary,

"He's asking if she was pissed, if she was a drinker . . . isn't that what you're asking? Then he puts that in his report and hey . . . no money."

I reassessed Peg, the hard stare, the fuck-you body language, and figured I could play. Said,

"So was she? Fond of it I mean? Being a student, it's part of the deal, best days of your life and all that."

She dropped the cig in her cup, swirled the contents, the fizzle making a noise like rumour. She said,

"You're a prick, you know that?"

I was warming to Peg, no doubt about it. Mary picked up a book, deciding I no longer mattered, asked Peg,

"You get to read this yet?"

I saw the title, *The Lovely Bones,* by Alice Sebold. It begins:

"My name was Salmon, like the fish; first name, Susie. I was fourteen when I was murdered."

Peg gave a dramatic shrug, went,

"I don't do saccharine shit."

Mary turned to me, explained,

"Susie, in the book, she was murdered. Our Sarah died in a freak accident, so pay the fucking money."

Before I could gear up, Peg went,

"Didn't I read an interview in the *Guardian* with Alice Sebold?"

Mary gave a smile of sheer malevolence. She'd been waiting for a male audience to run this by.

Here I was.

She didn't rub her hands in glee but it was there, in the neighbourhood. She began,

"Alice was eighteen, a student, and on her way home she was raped. Her attacker raped her with his fist and his penis, he beat her up and urinated on her face. When she got home that night, her father asked if she'd like something to eat."

Mary paused, so I knew this was going to be rough. She continued,

"Alice replied, 'That would be nice, considering the only thing I've had in my mouth in the last twenty-four hours is a cracker and a penis.'"

For once in my dumb life, I did the smart thing: I did nothing. They stared with expectation and I stared back.

Then Peg said,

"If there's nothing else . . . Mr? . . . we'd like to get on with other stuff, like our lives."

I stood up. God knows I'd been dismissed by experts. I had certainly been dissed. I asked,

"Might I see a copy of the book?"

Mary, suspicious, went,

"Alice Sebold?"

I watched their faces, said,

"A copy of a book by Synge, lying beneath the body."

Peg shrugged, began to build another coffee. I was wondering how wired she was going to get.

She said,

"It's in the bookcase . . . like . . .'cause . . . it's where we keep . . . books."

She enunciated this slowly like you would to a very slow child, but hey, I can do the tolerance rap. I asked,

"Might I see it?"

Mary stormed out, leaving me with the caffeined fiend. A few moments later she was back, held out the volume, asked,

"I give you this, are you gone?"

"Like the Midlands' wind."

I put it in my pocket, said,

"You've been most generous with your time."

Peg brushed past me, not quite shouldering me but the intention was clear, and she said,

"Wanker."

On that note, I was out of there.

I held off examining the volume till later, took a long walk out to the bay, bought a burger, large Coke and sat on the rocks. I refused to think about Ann Henderson, wished I had brought my Walkman. I hadn't yet moved along to Discmans and, like some dinosaur, was still using cassettes. There is one benefit: they slide on your belt like a smooth untruth.

Then and there I'd have listened to Bruce and *Empty Sky*. That he'd finally released a new album should have been great news. Here's the madness—and admitting it doesn't dilute the insanity—

"You need booze, dope for music."

Sorry, I need them. It's the illusion. A bottle of Jack, six pack of Lone Star and then . . . you're ready to rock. A cup of tea doesn't do it. Johnny Duhan, the soundtrack to my life, also had a new album, and I'd heard 'Inviolate', the best song on grief ever. Forget Iris de Ment with the song on her dad or Peter Gabriel's 'I Grieve' . . . here is THE SONG. It didn't lash me; it plain out lacerated.

I lit a cig and dwelt for a moment on a time with my father. We'd stand on these very rocks and cast for mackerel. Those times, the whole town was strung out along the bay, the fish literally surrendering. We took home eight and my mother threw them in the garbage.

Paulo Coelho in *Warriors of Light* writes,

"The warrior of light sometimes wonders why he's encountering the same set of problems over and over—then realises that he has never progressed past them, which is why the lesson keeps returning to teach him what he does not wish to learn."

I did not then, and probably not even now, want to know what drove my mother. I suspect it was rage, but as to where that came from or why, I didn't want to know.

Since her stroke, she'd had a live-in nurse. Then a kidney infection landed her in the hospital. At my last visit, strained as usual, her speech had greatly improved, a catheter had been inserted, and I tried not to stare. She said,

"I was able to use the commode by myself."

Heartbreaking, right?

To hear a tough-spirited woman boast of being able to use the toilet.

Wrong.

I thought,

"Tough shit!"

No pun intended and I rarely do irony, least not sober.

I took a last gulp of the bay and turned towards town, the final line of Padraig Pearse's poem . . . sorrowful. Stopped at Grattan Road and felt a melancholy as deep as false memory. Remember the massive hit Foreigner had with 'I Want to Know What Love Is'? On a rock nostalgia programme, I caught the version with the gospel choir singing shotgun. Man, that rocked. I was humming it all the way through the Claddagh.

Evening was in and at the hotel I nodded at Mrs Bailey. She said,

"My, you look healthy, a glow in your cheeks."

Windburn.

She handed me an envelope, said,

"I don't know who left it. I wasn't at the desk when it came."

On the front was "Jack Taylor". Typed. I opened it, read,

"Jack, can you meet me at 9 p.m. at the Fair Green?"

"Look at him and you're peering down a hole that needs to be filled but never will be."

Andrew Pyper, *The Trade Mission*

Upstairs, I read the note more fully:

Jack,

Can you meet me at 9 p.m. in the Fair Green? I'll be waiting where the City Link coaches park.

Ann

My heart was pounding, sweat breaking out on my brow. I'd have massacred a double Jameson. Had told myself a thousand times, "You're so over her." . . . Sometimes, I'd even believed it. Once to Jeff, I said,

"I'm over Ann."

He'd been stocking the bar, paused, asked,

"You give her the acid test?"

"What?"

"That's when you see her with a guy, he's got his arm round her, she's smiling up at him and you watch them, feel OK. That happens, you're over her."

I'd made some smart-ass reply. Course, I'd never seen her thus and prayed I never would. Obviously, I'd have failed. Tests were never my strong point, especially if they involved character.

I showered, shaved and laid out a pair of Farah, marvelling at the crease. Then figured, go for broke and wear a sports jacket. Had bought it in Age Concern. It was a lightweight navy wool job and fit like a metaphor. Transferring my keys, change, wallet from the other jacket, I found the book. Shit, I'd completely forgotten it. It was *The Collected Plays and Poems,* and I could tell it had almost never been opened. The title page had two words written in black ink:

THE DRAMATIST

I flipped through the pages. Typed on a label stuck onto the last page was: "Maura can at last look forward to the great rest." I could safely say I knew nothing about the plays or the poems, and precious little about Synge. Save that he lived a long time on the Aran Islands and convinced the world that stage Irish was a reality. I put it on top of the bookcase, and maybe I'd even read it, but not any time soon. Got dressed and checked myself in the mirror. Looking sharp. Asked aloud,

"Hot date, fellah?"

You bet.

Before I left the room, from nowhere, a vivid memory resurfaced.
I loved my father, admired, hero-worshipped; all of the textbook stuff.

I still do.

He taught me how to play snooker, hurling. He was a father of the old school. He did the unheard-of thing: he gave me his time, not in a hurried or impatient way but as if he loved to do so. My first hurley, he made it, cut from the ash tree. He honed, polished, tested it for weeks on end.

In our new era of prosperity, when fatherhood consists of McDonald's, PlayStations and shitpiles of cash, he taught me the virtue of patience. Only once did I ever see him "lose it". With my mother he'd have been justified in a daily tirade, but he never reacted to her continuous verbal onslaught. Sad to say, but I'd have broken her back with the hurley.

I was maybe ten and our terrace house bore witness to constant street activity. My father was home from work, had taken off his boots, and a group of lads were horse-playing at the window. As many as fifteen, what would constitute a crowd fuck today.

One of them began hitting the window with his elbow. My mother, exasperated, said,

"For heaven's sake."

And went out, asked them to move it along. Normally, that would be it, done deal. But the elbow one answered,

"Fuck off, you oul' bitch."

My father straightened in his chair. He glanced briefly at me, a look of such sadness in his eyes. I'd been expecting rage.

My mother came storming in.

"Did you hear what that pup called me?"

My father stood, in his stockinged feet, then went up the stairs.

My mother called,

"What kind of man are you?"

I knew he was gone to get his shoes. She, as usual, knew him not at all. A few moments later, he came down, his face set in stone, opened the door, closed it quietly. Through the window, we watched him wade through them, approach the elbow one, ask,

"What did you say to my wife?"

The fellah repeated it, bravado lighting up his face. I saw my father sigh, may even have heard it. Then, his whole body tensed, the strength compressing into the length of his right arm, and wallop, he dropped the guy like a stunned cow. He stared at the crumpled boy at his feet, seemed to make a tormented decision, then turned away.

The gang of lads, silent, moved out of his way. He strode into the kitchen, turned on the cold tap. As the water poured over the raw bleeding knuckles, he looked at me, his face in deep anguish, said,

"Jack, that was a response but it is never a solution."

I didn't agree with him then and I don't agree with him now. More wallops and we'd need less therapy.

Niall O'Shea was the lad with the smart mouth. My father had fractured his jaw. There were no repercussions, at least not of the legal kind. Unless you count my mother's comment,

"What sort of carry-on is that?"

Or the personal cost to my father. Over the next few years, I'd often meet Niall and he'd give me a sheepish smile. When I was a young guard, pulling night duty in Portumna, I was given four days' leave and ended up drinking in Hughes' in Woodquay. I met Niall in the crowded saloon and he bought me a pint. He was in the building game and making money, all on the "lump", he said,

"Did you know my jaw was wired for six months?"

I had a feed of drink but not enough to feel real comfortable with this conversation, went,

"Oh."

He was nodding, animated,

"Had to eat through a straw and, man, the frigging pain of it."

I gave a non-committal shrug and he shouted a fresh round, said,

"Your old man, he sure packed a punch."

Fitting epitaph.

It was the last time I saw Niall O'Shea. What I remember most is a very bad singer, murdering Johnny McEvoy's "Mursheen Durkin". It's an awful song anyway and needs no help with the cringe factor. Overlooking Galway docks, there's a massive crane that has blighted the landscape for a long time. Visible from any location in the city, it says everything you need to say about "urban renewal". A few years after our meeting, Niall O'Shea scaled that crane and jumped. He judged the position poorly as he missed the water and hit the concrete. Not even a straw was needed to scoop up what remained. I can never listen to Johnny McEvoy since, and I'm not blaming him. This is Irish logic; it never adds up.

I recount all this to demonstrate how preoccupied I was. If I'd been thinking clearly, I'd have focused on *where* Ann had asked to meet. A car park, at night? You have to figure I deserved what was rolling down the wire. Went out the door with Emily Dickinson's words as mantra:

"The heart wants what it wants

Or else it does not care."

Yeah.

Mrs Bailey gave a gasp of delight, said,

"My oh my, if I were fifty years younger, I'd give you a run for your money."

I was mortified, so kept it light, went,

"Ary, you're too much woman for me."

When she laughed, it came from her soul. You saw the woman who had weathered eighty years, who had witnessed her country dragged screaming into a prosperity that damn near destroyed all she believed in. She gave the stock reply of a satisfied Irish woman:

"Go on outta that."

Smothered in warmth, these words launched manys the Irish male upon an unsuspecting world. I swear there was bounce in my step as I walked along the arse end of the square. Both my legs working strong and healthy.

"The one consistent interest, passion and obsession of her life was books—even on the night of the fire. While people had often disappointed her, books never did. She was seldom without a stack of ten or more unread library books; a hedge against the reality she could not face."

Ann Rule, *Bitter Harvest*

I reached the Fair Green, moved to where the Dublin coaches
park. No sign of Ann. Two buses were lined near the wall,
a space between them. I walked along that, turned to see a
man blocking my path. He was big, dressed in a tracksuit, a
hurley held lightly in his left hand. He smiled, not with
humour or warmth but with a definite air of malevolence.
I said,

"Tim Coffey."

He nodded, answered,

"My wife won't be coming. Shame, seeing as you are all
fancied up, even got a frigging tie. Going to take her some-
where special, were you? Then ride her after? Was that
your plan?"

Spittle leaked from the corner of his mouth. I tried to
remember what I knew of him. He'd been a sergeant just
before I lost my job. Even then, he had a reputation for ferocity. Used his fists for the most trivial offence. The guards

were changing; constant media scrutiny, public awareness, all had forced them to tidy up their act. But men like him, who employed brutal methods, were secretly admired and always protected. Plus, he'd been a hurler of some promise, had turned out for provincial teams. There, too, his temper had short-circuited his sporting future.

I let my hands, palms upwards, stand out from my sides, to signal

"Hey, I'm cool, I don't want aggravation."

He swung the hurley, catching my right knee with a sickening smack. The pain was immediate, white heat searing to my brain, proclaiming,

"This is going to hurt like a son of a bitch."

It did.

I fell against the coach, sliding to the ground. Wish I could say I behaved in the macho mode and simply gritted my teeth. No, I howled like a banshee. He swung the hurley again, shattering the bridge of my nose. Then, as the blood cascaded down my white shirt, he flung the hurley aside, bent down, said,

"I'm a hands-on kind of guy."

And began to beat the shit out of me. I could smell his breath. He'd been wolfing curry recently and chasing it with Guinness and Jameson. Vomit mixed with my blood and I passed out. What I remember is that his nails were filthy, deep dirt entrenched, and I thought,

"Disgusting bastard."

I opened my eyes and flinched, expecting pain. There was none.
But I felt confined as if I was in a tight shroud. When I got
my bearings I realised I was in hospital, sun streaming
through the windows. My hearing hadn't kicked in and I
stared, in a soundless state. The ward was on full go, maybe
fifteen other beds, with nurses, visitors and patients
mouthing words I couldn't hear. I began to sit up and, like
a switch being turned, I could hear.

Too much.

Coming in stereo, like a wave of terror. I tried to cover
my ears.

A nurse appeared, said,

"You're back."

She fluffed my pillows because nurses have a moral obligation to do this twenty times daily, said,

"Now, you don't worry, I'll get the doctor."

Worry about what for Chrissakes? She returned with a

babe from *Baywatch*. No kidding, this doctor had the regulation white coat, but everything else was supermodel territory. Plus, she looked all of sixteen.

I couldn't help it, went,

"You're a doctor?"

Gorgeous smile. She'd had this reaction before, especially from beat-up old men. She answered,

"I'm Dr Lawlor. How are you feeling?"

"Confused . . . and thirsty."

She picked up my chart, said,

"You sustained a very severe beating. The guards will want to interview you. Your nose was broken . . ."

She paused, gave me an intense look, continued,

"But this is not the first time. Your nose has been broken before. Were you a rugby player?"

"Hardly."

She wasn't happy with my tone, but her happiness was way down on my list of priorities. When I said nothing further, she said,

"You have some broken ribs and you may experience difficulty breathing. Your right knee was severely damaged. We have inserted a pin. It's very possible you may have a slight limp. However, physio will ease this."

I wanted a cigarette . . . and a drink. But mostly I wanted out, asked,

"When can I leave?"

She smiled, asked,

"Pressing business?"

"Yeah."

She scanned the chart again, said,

"I don't see why you shouldn't be ready in a week."

It was five days. The first time I got out of bed, I nearly fell over. A shard of pain from my knee rocked through my system. I gobbled painkillers, told the nurses that sleep was difficult and got sleepers.

They worked.

Jeff came to visit, bearing grapes. I said,

"I hate grapes."

He looked the same as ever, like a half-assed hippy. Long grey hair pulled in a ponytail, black 501s, waistcoat and well-worn boots. He should have seemed ridiculous but he carried it off. His movements had a stoned languor and he never touched dope. He settled in the chair and I asked,

"How's the baby?"

"The baby is nearly three and still not walking. You have to go that extra mile with Down's syndrome, you know what I'm saying?"

I didn't.

Initially, he had been near destroyed with his daughter's handicap. Now though, he had a handle on it. He asked, indicating my condition,

"This related to a case?"

I considered laying it out for him, he was my friend, but went,

"No, it was personal."

He digested that and I began to ease out of bed. He rose to help and I said,

"No, I've got to do this myself."

A brief smile and he replied,

"Like everything else . . . you're the last of the independents, like Walter Mathau in *Charly Varrick*."

Walking was a bastard. They'd given me a frame but I refused to use it. Started to hobble out of the ward, Jeff walking point. I saw the nurses stare at him; he wasn't unlike a Hell's Angel, cleaned up for court. He did own a Harley, the soft-tail custom. Halfway down the corridor, there's an alcove with signs warning:

NO SMOKING.

Three patients trailing IVs were huddled there, smoking like troopers. You could barely see them through the blue haze.

Jeff said,

"Tell me we're not sitting here."

I sat.

Jeff sighed, asked,

"Can't we go someplace private?"

The patient beside me had yellow skin, thin as mist, and when he inhaled, his cheekbones disappeared. I asked,

"Spare one, pal?"

He nodded, rummaged in his dressing gown, took out a crushed pack of Players, the old box with the sailor on the front. I didn't think they made them any more. I took one, smoothed out the creases, tapped it on my wrist to shake the loose tobacco and put it in my mouth. The man produced a brass Zippo, lit me up. I stared at the lighter, said,

"I'd one of them once."

He grunted, answered,

"It will see me out. I've cancer and no visitors."

What do you reply . . . bummer?

I turned to Jeff, coughed as the nicotine hit, and he said,

"I can hear you're enjoying that."

"Yeah."

Jeff leaned closer, said,

"If you need any back-up with . . ."

He indicated my injuries.

"I'm here for you."

I looked at him in astonishment, said,

"You! You're kidding! Since when did you do muscle?"

A note of derision in my voice and he caught it, said,

"I ride a Harley. You learn how to take care of things."

I stubbed at the cig, said,

"Thanks, Jeff, but it's over, it was a one-off."

He wasn't convinced. The lunch trollies were being prepared, and he put out his hand, we shook, and he added,

"You can't go on living like this."

I didn't have an answer and watched as he walked away. Back at the ward, someone had stolen the grapes.

"Around me the world seemed to slip sideways and all the things in the room suddenly looked flat and sharply defined, like high resolution photos of themselves that were too intensely concentrated to recognize. I stood in a synaptic freeze and catalogued my idiocy."

Matthew Stokoe, *High Life*

The guards came, interviewed me briefly. They at least had the grace to look ashamed as we went through the ritual. My song veered between "I don't know" and "Don't remember." They chorused with "We'll continue with our inquiries."

I received get-well cards from Mrs Bailey, Janet, Cathy. The day before my release, I was in the alcove and sucking on a cigarette, looked up and there was Tim Coffey. I felt a shudder but he put out his hand. I asked,

"Where's your hurley?"

He gave a knowing grin, said,

"I'm prepared to let bygones be bygones. What do you say, shake?"

My mouth had gone dry else I'd have spat on his outstretched hand.

He glanced at my leg, went,

"I hear you'll have a limp. Jack the gimp, the kids will shout after you; little fuckers, they can be so cruel."

In as level a voice as I could, I said,

"I'll have a limp and you, you'll have something to think about."

It threw him slightly, but he moved his shoulders, adjusting his body weight, asked,

"And what would that be?"

"When I'm coming."

There was no card from Ann. I watched the news. An oil spill at the docks, endangering the swans and the oyster beds. I heard someone call,

"Jack Taylor?"

Turned to face Fr Malachy, my mother's friend. We had years of warfare. He surveyed my condition, said,

"The drink no doubt."

"I haven't had a drink for six months."

"A likely story—you'll never draw a sober breath."

I stood, as you never want a man like him to have any advantage. The smell of stale cigarettes came off him in waves. He was wearing the black suit, dandruff on the shoulders, like a sinister jackdaw. The dog collar was grubby, and you wanted to stuff him in a washing machine, turn to mega cycle. I asked,

"They have you nurturing to the sick?"

He glanced around the ward, distaste writ large, said,

"Nobody wants the clergy any more, except the old bid-

dies who try to grab your hand, ask you can you get Padre
Pio's glove."

"Saint."

"What?"

"St Padre Pio. He was canonised during the World
Cup . . . the day Spain beat us on the penalties."

"They should never have sent Roy home."

I wasn't going to open that can of worms. Not since the
shooting of Michael Collins had the country been so di-
vided. You either backed Roy Keane or you didn't. Even
Northern Ireland didn't arouse the same passions. Malachy
gave a deep groan, the signal for nicotine. I have never
known anyone as addicted as him. He'd light one from the
butt of another. The urge was on him now and with ferocity. I began to walk down the ward and he followed, whin-
ing,

"Hey, I haven't finished."

"You'll want a smoke, right?"

"So?"

"So, even priests have to obey the rules . . . well, the blatant ones anyway."

At the alcove, the huddled smokers chorused,

"Father."

He ignored them, grabbed my arm tightly, and I said,

"Back off."

He didn't, went,

"Your mother had to be moved to a nursing home. She's

paralysed on one side and requires twenty-four hour nursing."

She'd hate that, had said once:

"Nursing home? Knacker's yard more like. Once you go in, you never come out. Promise me, son, promise me you'll never let that happen."

I never promised, but my father would turn in his grave so I asked,

"Where is it?"

"Grattan Road, called St Jude's."

He released my arm, seemed uncomfortable, so I pushed,

"Is it OK?"

He stubbed his cigarette on the floor, ashtrays all round him, said,

"It's a bit basic. She doesn't have a lot of money, but well, life is hard."

One of the smokers moved forward, asked,

"Father, could you give us a blessing?"

"Don't annoy me."

He hissed and stomped off.

The hospital had cleaned my clothes, but the bloodstains still clung faintly to the shirt. I looked bedraggled. To ease my limp, they'd given me a walking stick. I'd refused but had to relent. Leaning on it, I thanked the nurse, got a supply of painkillers and took the elevator to the ground floor. A fortune had been spent on the hospital foyer and spent recklessly. It looks like the departure lounge of an airport, with a flash coffee bar, massive potted plants and an air of opulence. Nobody can find Admissions, and people wander round in dazed confusion.

I phoned a taxi and the girl said,

"It will be about twenty minutes. How will the driver know you?"

"I'll be in the coffee bar, I have a cane . . ."

And before I could continue, she roared,

"Five nine, pick up at the hospital, an old guy with a walking stick."

Click.

Tried not to think about that, got a coffee and eased myself carefully into the chair, heard,

"Jack!"

Turned to see Ann Henderson approaching. My heart lurched. She was wearing cord boot-cut pants with a tight yellow sweater, the sleeves rolled back, showing a light tan. Her wedding band seemed to shine. She asked,

"May I sit?"

"Sure."

As usual, the very sight of her brought a lump to my throat. I'd hung the handle of the cane on the rim of the table, and she glanced quickly at it. I said,

"I've just been described as an old guy."

That hurt her and I felt a twinge of pleasure. Christ, I wanted to hurt her badly. She answered,

"I am so desperately sorry."

"Why, because I'm old?"

Shook her head, vague annoyance for a moment, then,

"For what happened to you."

"You didn't do it."

"I caused it. I told Tim about our meeting, and so he wrote the note to you out of jealousy."

And then,

"But I didn't know about the note until after you were hurt."

I let that hang there. If she'd hoped for understanding, I was all out. I put the spoon in my coffee, stirred madly.

She moved her hand to touch me and I snapped,

"Don't you dare."

She recoiled as if bitten. I said,

"He came to see me, your husband. Without grapes or even a hurley, but he did want to let bygones be bygones. What do you think, Ann? Should I let it go, maybe get a mass said, and every time I limp, I could like, offer it up for the souls in purgatory. Do you think that's the way to go?"

Her face was contorted in pain, as every word I slowly uttered lashed her deeper. She took a deep breath, asked,

"Jack, could you . . . could you let it go?"

"No."

She was wringing her hands, then,

"If you harm him, I'll never see you again. You'll be dead to me."

A man walked up, asked,

"You called for a taxi?"

I nodded, stood and reached for my cane. She shot her hand out, touched mine, pleaded,

"I'm begging, Jack."

I leant in close, her perfume causing a dance in my head, said,

"Give your husband a message, can you do that? Tell him his hurling days are over."

I limped after the taxi driver, who asked,

"You need some help there, buddy?"

I shook my head. The help I needed only came with a Jameson seal. When I was settled in the back, he got the car in gear, swore at an ambulance and we moved. Eyed me in the mirror, asked,

"That your missus?"

"No, that's my past."

Digesting that, he turned the radio on. I recognised Lyric FM, the classical station. The announcer said,

"That of course was Arvo Part, 'tabula rasa', and later we'll have 'Festina Lente'."

I muttered,

"I bet you bloody will."

"But this was no ordinary AA group. The failed, the aberrant, the doubly addicted and the totally brain fried whose neuroses didn't even have a name found their way to the 'work the steps or die motherfucker meeting'."

James Lee Burke, *Jolie Blon's Bounce*

Mrs Bailey made a huge fuss on seeing me, went,

"Oh, by the holy, look at the state of you."

She wanted to move me to a room on the ground floor because of my leg, but I was having none of that. I loved where I was, said,

"The exercise is good. I need to keep moving."

Janet, the chambermaid, burst out crying, threw her arms round me, wailed,

"We thought you'd been killed."

I went with the saying of my youth, the defence against emotion, said,

"Sure, you can't kill a bad thing."

I could feel her tears soak through my shirt and was more affected than I'd ever admit. Here, if fragmented, if ancient in years, was family.

She finally released me, said,

"And all the weight you've lost, you're like a Biafran."

To a certain generation in Ireland, despite the number of world famines since, Biafra remains the reference, maybe because for the first time we saw up close the ravages of another country. Famine is the wound that moulded our psyche. I finally got to my room and closed the door with a sigh of relief. Janet had placed a bouquet of flowers on my bookcase and a box of Dairy Milk.

Chocolates.

It made me smile. I'd have killed for a bottle of Jameson and she'd given me sweets.

The Sacred Heart calendar was still there, so I checked what nugget of wisdom was on offer, muttering,

"Better be awesome."

"Lord, set my heart free."

So it was true, God did have a sense of humour, even if his timing was off. I lit a cig and turned on the radio. Bush was saying he had to bomb Iraq for his daddy, and John Major was playing down the revelation of his four-year affair with Edwina Currie. Then the local news: a schoolgirl had been attacked on her way to school. She was eleven. In broad daylight, a man had dragged her into an alley. He was still at large but a massive hunt was underway. I went to make coffee and almost missed the next item. A female student had fallen down a flight of steps, been killed instantly. I froze, the coffee filter in my hand, said,

"What?"

There were no more details. The weather forecast predicted rain and the chance of thunder. My knee ached and

I checked the medication I'd received from the hospital. Six painkillers. Jeez, I could have done three right then, hit the cloud of unknowing. Took one, washed it down with the coffee, got out my address book, found the number, dialled, heard,

"Hello?"

"Bríd?"

"Who is this?"

"Jack Taylor."

She was not happy to hear my name, went,

"You called me by my Christian name. Usually it's 'Ridge', knowing I hate the English form."

She was going to put me through my paces, so I got my responses primed, said,

"OK, let's start over, Nic an Iomaire. There, does that score any points?"

Long pause. I debated asking how Margaret, her "friend", was, but felt it wouldn't further my cause, so I waited till,

"Are you still in hospital?"

"I'm out you'll be glad to hear, and if not good as new, at least I'm full of fire. Thanks for taking the time to visit. How did you know?"

I pictured her having the vexed look; I'd seen it often enough. She seemed for ever on the verge of punching me out and, God forgive me, I got a buzz out of needling her. She was such a what the Americans call "tight ass". Now she went,

"A guard half kills an ex-guard, you think every guard in the country doesn't know?"

My turn at vexation, asked,

"Then how come your colleagues who interviewed me appeared baffled?"

She didn't hesitate,

"Wake up and smell the coffee."

If it was meant to irritate, it worked. My teeth clenched and I counted to ten, then,

"I'll bet you have wanted to say that for a long time."

Now she was impatient.

"Did you want something? This is hardly a social call."

"The student who fell down the steps, do you know any details?"

She was angry, her breath coming rapidly, asked,

"Are you trying to be a private eye again? Surely you've learnt your lesson by now?"

I didn't want her usual lecture, cut in,

"I just need to know one detail, can you find that out?"

"Go on."

"When the girl was found, was there anything under her body?"

I could hear her intake of breath and I pressed,

"There was, Jesus . . . wasn't there?"

An age before she answered, then,

"It's complicated."

"I can do complicated, try me."

"If this gets out . . . OK, I'm friendly with one of the

uniforms who was first on the scene. He picked up a book . . ."

"The stupid fuck."

I could hear her reeling it in, trying to regain her edge. I recognised it as it's a place I inhabit a lot. The radio was still playing and I heard the DJ announce an Elvis Costello song, 'I Want You', from the album *Blood and Chocolate.* The track was nasty, mean, angry, but disguised as something lighter. What you'd expect from a late-forties, white, divorced male. It seemed to suck all the air out of the room. Ridge said,

"He knows he screwed up."

"Get the book."

"What?"

"Get the frigging book from him. Are you deaf?"

"Is that an order?"

"It's absolutely vital."

And I hung up.

I was half sorry I hadn't mentioned the headline on *The Sentinel*:

BISHOP BANS GAY WEDDINGS

At St Nicholas's, the Protestant church, a gay wedding had taken place. Their bishop was now stepping in. As children, so conditioned by Catholicism were we that we hurried past that church lest its tentacles reach out and grab us. Even now, when I pass there, I quicken my pace.

The room had closed in and I had to get out. An obses-

sion for Jameson had lodged in my brain. I took the stairs
down, and with the cane it was a slow, awkward business.

Mrs Bailey appeared perturbed, said,

"Shouldn't you be resting?"

"Exercise is the best thing."

She stabbed her finger at the newspaper before her. I
knew it was the *Irish Independent,* as it had been all her life.
It showed your political colours as clear as a banner. She
said,

"The Nice Referendum, what does the government
think? They can keep calling them till they get the result
they want?"

Politics was the furthest thing from my mind, but I had
to show some spunk, tried,

"I take it you'll be voting no?"

As is the Irish way, she immediately avoided the issue
with,

"Them Orange bastards have stitched up Sinn Féin,
raided their offices in Stormont."

I was taken aback, marvelling at her choice of words.
She was over eighty, as old Galway as the Spanish Arch. I
asked,

"Stitched up? Good Lord, where did you learn that?"

"I watch *The Bill* and *Eastenders.*"

"I thought you were a *Coronation Street* fan?"

"Not since Hilda Ogden left."

That's a conversation killer right there. I nodded and
said,

"See you later."

It was strange being out, back in public. Hospital has its own complete world, and I wasn't sure it wasn't more appealing.

A priest crossed the street, said,

"How are you?"

Jeez, I was up to me eyes in clergy. He looked vaguely familiar but I couldn't place him. He asked,

"What happened to you?"

"A rugby accident."

Stick it to him, he'd be GAA . . . they all were. He seemed confused, then put it together, said,

"Oh, I see. I actually was referring to mass, to your attendance. I haven't seen you for a while."

The word "attendance" was one of my triggers. Even in my days as a guard, I was poor at regulation. I asked,

"What, you're marking my card?"

He was surprised and tried to rally.

"Good Lord, I put that badly. What I meant was we missed you."

I wanted to grab him by the collar, shake him and scream "wake up". I said,

"Sure you did."

He did the religious bit of turning his cheek, ignored my tone and said,

"No doubt we'll be seeing you this Sunday?"

"And pigs might fly."

I turned on my heel and limped away.

"People I knew had turned out to be strange and savage. They had hung Mose and kicked and hit me and my father."

Joe R. Lansdale, *The Bottoms*

Near Eyre Square I saw the young blond guy, and no mistake, he was staring at me. I decided to put an end to this and moved, but he turned and was gone before I could reach him. I swore that next time, one way or another, I was going to have a chat. I mean, what the hell, was he stalking me?

I got into Nestor's, visions of whiskey before my eyes. The sentry was in place, said,

"Jaysus, look at the cut of him."

This is not complimentary; it's as bad as it gets. I shot him a look.

Jeff was stocking shelves, said,

"Welcome back, buddy."

I took my usual chair, the hard one, my back to the wall. Felt tired, my knee aching; the damn painkiller wasn't kicking in. The news was on: a bomb in Bali, 187 dead, three Irish missing. The newsreader was speculating on Al-Qaeda involvement. Jeff brought over a pot of coffee, two mugs. I felt a flash of anger, the presumption I wasn't drinking made me want to roar. Jeff paused, asked,

"Coffee OK?"

"Sure, just what the doctor ordered. You're joining me?"

"If you don't mind, I need a word."

I waved my hand, indicating the empty chair. He sat, poured two fills. Despite myself, I responded to the caffeine aroma. Maybe I'd drink later, live on the expectation.

The sentry asked,

"Want to get in the pool?"

"Pool?"

"Yeah, for five euro, pick a date that Bush will bomb Iraq. November fifth, fifteenth and twenty-fifth are gone."

I gave it a bit of thought, said,

"November twentieth."

The sentry made a note in a small red book, said,

"There's a fair whack going to be in it; everybody wants to play."

I got a five out of my wallet and left it on the table. Jeff asked,

"You heard about the schoolgirl?"

"Being attacked, you mean?"

He nodded. Now that he had a daughter, he'd be particularly sensitive to this. But as usual, I was wrong. I'd jumped yet again to the wrong conclusion. He said,

"There's a guy I know, Pat Young, we've been friends . . ."

I put up my hand to shush him. The radio had kicked in

and Jimmy Norman was playing Emmylou Harris, my favourite track from *Red Dirt Girl* . . . "Bang the Drum Slowly". Kills me. Jeff waited till it was through and I asked,

"You were saying?"

"Pat's a good guy. He's not had it easy. In Bohermore they have a different take on sobriety. They stop drinking and get a bike. Not your textbook therapy but it works for Pat."

My eyes strayed to the top shelf. Whiskey, brandy, eeny, meeney . . . vodka schnapps . . . miney, mo. Tequila, now there was something that did the job, fast, ruthless and efficient. I heard Emmylou's lyric "Meant to ask you about the war" and snapped,

"There's a point to this story?"

He was surprised, physically jerked back, said,

"Pat might be in the frame."

"For what?"

"For the schoolgirl."

I took a moment, got my head in gear, asked,

"How did that happen?"

Jeff ran his hand through his hair, deep lines across his forehead. When did they happen? He said,

"Pat was seen in the vicinity . . . And the girl knows him."

Time to cut to the chase. I asked,

"What's that mean? Knows him . . . what am I supposed to infer?"

"She asked him for money one time, for ice cream, and he refused."

I didn't see the problem, said,

"DNA will clear him, no big deal."

Jeff was shaking his head, said,

"I don't think an actual rape happened. The guards are under enormous pressure to get a result. The likes of Pat, he'll do nicely."

I raised my hands, had enough, said,

"Sad story, but shit happens."

Now Jeff had reached the pass, stalled, then,

"I was hoping, you know, with your contacts, you could maybe make a few inquiries, put a good word in."

I was truly amazed. Jeff wasn't a guy to beg, to ask for a favour, but here he was, pleading for something. I wish I could say I was gracious, that I leaped at the chance to dig out my friend. No. I said,

"Aren't you the guy always busting my balls, saying I have to give up the investigation business? Hell, you're for ever expressing concern for my well-being, for my sobriety."

The last word I lashed, then deliberately pushed the coffee cup aside.

Jeff took a deep breath, then,

"There's talk of a vigilante group in the town, and I'm afraid they might target Pat."

I let my face register ridicule, and he sighed; disappointment coursed through his body. He pushed back the chair, gathered the mugs, shrugged, said,

"Forget I asked."

Immediately I felt bad. Fuck, I wanted to score a point, not annihilate him, tried,

"Jeez, Jeff, take it easy, I didn't say I wouldn't help. Did I say that?"

His face showed how much he wanted to tell me to shove it, but concern for Pat Young overrode his personal bile. I could see the conflict, the turmoil in his eyes. He squared his shoulders, said,

"OK, anything you can do . . . would be . . . deeply appreciated."

I'd made him jump through hoops and I regretted it. Blame my knee, blame the clergy who'd been in my face, blame the fact I wanted to drink till I howled. The truth is I behave badly more often than I dare admit. I stood up, trying for damage limitation, went,

"I'll get right on it."

He gave me an odd look, asked,

"You ever hear of the Pikemen?"

I rummaged through the haphazard store of Irish history, tried,

"1798, the rebellion—weren't they some sort of secret society?"

He turned to the bar, then,

"The Pikemen I mean aren't history."

Then he moved away.

I was coming along the square and the sun appeared. It almost felt warm. I sat near the fountain and tried to figure out the mess of data I had. Without doubt, I was suffering from information overload. Attempting to list my priorities, I had:

> The drug dealer
> His dead sister
> Synge
> Another dead student
> Another book?
> An abortive rape
> Jeff's friend

The drinking school was in full roar near what used to be the public toilets. After the paedophile scandal, the toilets had been demolished and replaced by metal booths that were pay-to-enter. A wino detached himself from the

group, approached. He had startling red hair, two teeth and
a heavy black coat. A French kerchief was knotted around
his neck. It lent him a raffish air. He gave me an ingratiat-
ing smile, his body language assuming the non-threatening
pose, said,

"Good day to you, sir."

English accent with a hint of Tyneside. Maybe it was the
sunshine, but the rage I'd been nourishing leaked away. I
answered,

"How are you doing?"

He was delighted. I could see his eyes estimating how
much my civility was worth. I got there first, asked,

"Where are you from?"

Took him a moment to regroup—money was his pri-
mary purpose, but a little banter might increase the tally—
then a frown as another thought hit. He asked,

"You're not a social worker, are you?"

I moved my cane to the other hand, said,

"Hardly."

His body relaxed and he sat beside me. The odour from
his clothes and body was a potent mix of urine, dirt, misery and Buckfast. I tried not to gag, and he said,

"I'm from Newcastle."

"You and Kevin Keegan."

"And Alan Shearer, don't forget him. He's a good one,
gave me a fiver once to mind his car."

"Why did you come to Galway?"

The question perplexed him. The school called to him,

impatience in their tone. He was taking far too long to score. The whole strategy was hit and run. I didn't really care why he'd come, but it was now vital to him. He screwed his eyes, then,

"I heard the government gives money for everything. If you have dogs, you can even claim for them."

I decided to save him the ritual and took out a few notes, handed them over. He quickly stowed them in his coat lest I change my mind, but principally so the school wouldn't see the amount. Loyalty is not a top item on the agenda of the street. Clouds began to move across the sky and I stood up.

He asked,

"If I may be so bold as to ask, what happened to your knee?"

"A guy beat me."

He knew that song and nodded, past beatings registering in his eyes. He looked all of twenty years old and he asked,

"Did you beat him in return?"

"Not yet."

He savoured that, and then I asked him,

"Why didn't you get a dog?"

"Oh, I did . . . I ate him."

"He had seen people who had hanged themselves, stuck a shotgun in their mouth or blown themselves to bits. Somehow he had learned to endure what he saw and put it aside."

Henning Mankell, *Sidetracked*

YES.

The vote was in and Ireland had ratified the Treaty of Nice. It was the first time we'd voted on a Saturday, the second time we'd voted on this issue. The way was now clear for expansion, and a slew of new countries could join the European Union. On Shop Street non-nationals were smiling and saying "Hello." Usually they kept their heads down, looked seriously depressed. I used to blame the weather.

I was en route to visit my mother. I stopped at Griffin's Bakery and bought an apple tart. As always, there was a queue. A man said,

"The Washington sniper hit again."

A flurry of speculation and, as is the Irish custom, talk switched back to politics. A woman said,

"That Nice Treaty, it will damage our neutrality."

Another older woman, silent till now, said, a note of wistfulness in her voice,

"Them Nice biscuits, they'd a grand bite."

Grattan Road has always been the poor relation of Salthill. It has a beach but the sewers run dangerously close. Even on the sunniest day, an air of greyness hangs over it. The nursing home was in a secluded street, way back from the sea. I had to ask for directions. An elderly man with a cloth cap was sitting on a bench, peering out at the horizon. When I asked him, I thought he didn't hear me and was about to repeat myself when he cleared his throat, spat a wad of phlegm dangerously close to my shoe. He said,

"You don't want to go there, son."

Son!

The ever-present rage, continually simmering, near surfaced. I wanted to shout,

"Listen, you dozy bastard, get with the game."

He looked at me, yellow tinges at the white of his eyes. His nose seemed to have collapsed. He asked,

"Know what age I am?"

Like I gave a fuck. I said,

"I've no idea."

He cleared his throat and I stepped clear but the hawking didn't follow. Maybe he had nothing left. He answered for me.

"Too bloody old, that's how old I am. I live with my

daughter, she hates me, I have to be out all day. Do you know how hard it is to kill time?"

I knew.

Then he shot his arm out, frayed cuffs beneath a check jacket and . . . cufflinks. How old is that? Finger pointing, he croaked,

"The kip you want is over that way, second turn on the right."

"Thanks."

I felt a need to reach out, touch his bony shoulder, offer some comfort. But what kind of lie could I peddle? I left the apple tart on the seat beside him but he ignored it.

He asked,

"You have family in that hole?"

"My mother."

He nodded, as if he'd heard all the awful stories. I turned to go and he said,

"Son."

"Yes?"

"You want to do your mother a favour?"

Did I?

Tried,

"Yes."

"Put a pillow over her head."

I'd met literally thousands of people, and that's allowing for Irish hyperbole. In my years on the force, I encountered every type of

> Trickster
> Con man
> Villain
> Rogue.

And the years after I met the

> Sad
> Lonely
> Depressed
> Dispirited.

But few reached me like that old man. A song stirred in my memory, an early Emmylou, where she wails, laments, "A River for Him".

If Johnny Duhan was the lyrics of my life, then she was the melody. As I approached the nursing home, my heart sank. It was the curtains on the front window. Hanging from a dropped rail, they were dull brown. As a man, I'm not really supposed to notice if they were clean.

I noticed.

They were lighting. That's a Bohermore expression, lighting with the dirt. The name, St Jude's, was on the door. The J had disappeared so it read:

"St ude's".

The patron saint of hopeless cases all right. I rang the bell, heard keys being turned. The sound was remarkably similar to Mountjoy. A middle-aged woman opened it, asked,

"Yes?"

Terse.

She had the severity expression down cold. If they were ever searching for a dominatrix, here she was. As if she'd simply moved right along from her previous incarnation as a warden at the Magdalen Laundry.

I said,

"I'm here to see Mrs Taylor."

She was wearing a heavy tweed suit, thick-soled black shoes that a nun would kill for, her hair held in some kind of mosquito net. The look in her eyes was icy and mea-sured. She asked,

"Who are you?"

"I'm her son."

She didn't scoff but came close. The door was still only half open and she rasped,

"You haven't been before?"

I wanted to shove the door, storm in. It went without saying this woman and I would never be friends, but even tense cordiality wasn't likely. I said,

"If I'd been here before, would we be having this conversation? But then, who knows? Maybe this rigmarole is a regular process."

There, the lines were drawn. This was a woman who didn't often get cheek or, as I felt she'd have put it, impertinence. I could see how close she was to slamming the door. I asked,

"So, can I see my mother or am I going to need a warrant?"

She gave my cane a look of scorn then opened the door, a mound of post at her feet. They looked like bills. The Final Demand variety. I'd seen enough to recognise the envelopes. I moved by her and the smell hit. A blend of ammonia, old clothes, urine and Wild Pine. The latter is the air freshener of choice in institutions. Sold by the truckload and made in Taiwan, it is cheap and odious. Once you've encountered it, you never mistake it for anything else. It has a cloying sweetness that sticks itself to everything. It's worse than any smell it poorly attempts to disguise. I remembered my first dances, in the showband era. Woolworth's had a branch on Eyre Square, now occupied by Supermac's. Their speciality was a sixpence bottle of perfume. Every house in town had claim to at least one bottle. The dancehalls were electric with the aroma.

I noticed a huge vase of flowers and put out my hand. Plastic.

Of all the horrors of commerce, these are among the worst. On a par with the three flying ducks that adorned the walls of a thousand households. I turned to her, asked,

"And you are?"

"Mrs Canty. I'm the matron."

I nodded as if I gave a toss. She said,

"Your mother is in room seven."

She seemed on the verge of more but stifled it, said,

"If you'll excuse me, the home won't run itself."

She stomped off, hostility trailing in her wake. I found room seven, the door open, and, taking a deep breath, I went in. Using my cane, I was no advertisement for the outside world. The room was dim because the bulb had the lowest voltage. Last time I experienced that was in my bedsit hovel on Ladbroke Grove, "Madame George" as my theme song.

There were three cots—you couldn't call them beds—metal frames pulled up alongside to keep the occupants in or help out, I didn't know. I approached the first, a woman of vast years, on her back, her mouth open, spit leaking from her mouth. The second held my mother. She was propped up on pillows, her eyes open. Since I'd last seen her, she had deteriorated to a huge degree. Her once lustrous black hair was white and lank. The eyes focused and she whispered,

"Jack?"

My heart was pierced, I wanted to weep. Guilt, rage and remorse tore through my stomach. I felt bile in my throat and the taste of actual vomit along my gums. I said,

"How are you doing?"

Not my finest moment. She lifted her hand, the arm as thin as paper, asked,

"Will you bring me home?"

Home. We had no home, never had. We'd lived in a house of seething hostility, all created by her. I said,

"Sure I will."

Her eyes were wild and moved furiously. She said,

"Move closer, Jack, they'll hear us. They'll say I'm not being a good girl."

I stayed twenty minutes, seemed twenty years. I kept repeating I'd rescue her. She was close to being what the Irish call *seafóid,* meaning a person soft in the head or, in modern terms, having lost it. When I was leaving, she said,

"Pray to Herself to save me."

The matron was unlocking the door. I said,

"An old man over there, he said this was a kip. He was seriously understating it."

She slammed the door behind me.

Sin scéal eile.

(That's another story.)

Back at Bailey's, I thought about Jeff's friend and decided there wasn't a whole lot I could do. I rationalised, if he was in-nocent, then he'd be OK. I didn't buy that shit for a minute but figured my involvement wouldn't help, so I did nothing. As for my mother, the only solution was another nursing home. I knew a decent one would be expensive, and I couldn't afford it. So again, I did nothing.

The phone rang and I leaped at the distraction. It was the ban garda. She opened,

"I got the book."

"Terrific. Can you drop it off here?"

No reply and I had to go,

"Ridge, you there?"

When she answered, her indignation was evident.

"What do you think, I'm your messenger boy?"

"No . . . I . . ."

"You always lay down the times, terms and locations of our meetings."

Did I?

I asked,

"Do I?"

She didn't bother to answer, said,

"It's my birthday. Margaret is treating me to dinner at the Connemara Coast Hotel. We'll be in the lounge after for coffee . . . say 9 P.M.?"

"But that's . . ."

"In Connemara, yes. You'll remember it's my home."

"It's miles out. How am I supposed to get there?"

I swear she was laughing. With relish she suggested,

"Take a bus. When they see the cane, you'll probably get half fare."

Click.

I'd lost that round hands down. There'd been a time when Ridge was deferential, nigh submissive. I'd definitely intimidated her. Like all the women I knew, time took care of any shaky power I had. I rang Bus Éireann, and after thirty minutes of numbing frustration, I got the timetable. I'd gone through that rigmarole of "for information push 1, for bookings push 2, for prepaid holidays push 3." There didn't seem to be a button for civility.

A song had been going round in my head that I couldn't identify. Put the radio on and, by one of those weird coincidences, here it was. By Pink, titled "Like a Pill". What it did was make me feel old. I'd no business listening to the "antidote" to Britney. Sometimes, you can have too much information. The news kicked in and the guards said a man had been helping with their inquiries on the attack on the young girl. He had been released without charge. I rang Jeff and he confirmed it was Pat and, yes, he'd been released. I said,

"No worries then."

He didn't answer and I asked,

"Jeff?"

He sounded strained, said,

"It's not the guards I'm worried about."

And hung up. I considered calling him back but let it go. That was one item I could cross off my list. The post came, delivered to my room by Janet, who said,

"Isn't it a miracle?"

"The post?"

"Aw, don't be pulling my leg. I mean about your drinking."

"Oh, right."

She gave me a warm smile, affection oozing from her, asked,

"Do you say your prayers, Mr Taylor?"

"Um, yes, of course, in Irish, too."

This wasn't a complete lie. When I'd said them, a long time ago, I had said them in Irish.

She handed me a leaflet, said,

"It's the November Dead List."

For a surreal moment, I thought she was telling me who

was due to die, then I realised it was outlining the dates for "Cemetery Sunday" and the list of special masses during the month. She said,

"So you can visit your loved ones. I know you miss them."

She had that right, then,

" 'Tis fierce weather."

And she was gone. I folded the leaflet, rolled it tight and lobbed it, forgot my bad knee and attempted a kick.

Bad idea.

Pain coursed along my thigh and I had to rest. If I was superstitious, and being Irish it comes with the territory, I'd have said it was punishment for mockery. I looked at the post—two letters. One saying I could avail of the opportunity to have a free meal at the Radisson if I filled in a loyalty card. The second was from a solicitor acting on behalf of Stewart and enclosing a substantial cheque. The tone of the letter suggested that if I wasn't satisfied, more funds were readily available. I was satisfied.

Settled my head on the pillow and tried not to think about my mother.

Focused on my new plan. Once it had been a flat near Hyde Park. That had gone down the toilet. Nelson Algren had long been one of my favourite writers. At the end of his life, after poverty, literary neglect, heartache, he finally settled in Sag Harbor. An old whaling town, he could get around on his bicycle, and New York was just a train ride away. The house he finally rented appealed greatly to me. Near the ocean, it was $375 a month. It had a small back-yard, a fireplace and room to display all the items he'd kept in storage for years. E.L. Doctorow lived nearby, Betty Friedan across the street, Kurt Vonnegut in the next town.

I had a yearly diary on my bookcase. Used it to keep a vague track of money and phone numbers. The rest of the pages were blank. I got a black felt pen, wrote:

"SAG HARBOR OR BUST."

Mad as the dream was, it made me feel good, as if I had a future.

The Sacred Heart calendar said:

"Be humble before the Lord."

I didn't know much about humility but I was well versed in humiliation.

I figured I'd buy a present for Ridge's birthday. What do you buy for a gay ban garda who dislikes you with intensity?

Barbed wire?

There's a corner shop close to the hotel. Despite its proximity, I'd avoided it for years. In my days as a guard, I'd had to caution the owner for overcharging. He hadn't responded well. He said,

"You pup, I gave your oul wan tick when she hadn't a pot to piss in."

Like that.

I fully expected he was still running the shop, but his carbon copy, the son, was behind the counter. I think we'd gone to school together. I said,

"Seamus."

He held up his hand to silence me. A gesture I'm not wild about. A news item that a young man had been found crucified in Belfast. He'd been so badly beaten that his own father didn't recognise him. Seamus reached over, turned the radio off, said,

"Jack Taylor, we don't usually get your business."

Already the bitter word. I wanted to say,

"What a surprise and you reeking in charisma."

Went with,

"How's your dad?"

"Dead, thanks."

Before I could rise to this reply, a non-national entered and Seamus was instantly on alert. As if a button had been pressed, his eyes narrowed and he snapped,

"Help you?"

The man was intimidated; he recognised the tone. Keeping his eyes down, he said,

"Some sugar, please?"

"Bottom shelf, next to the tea and coffee."

Seamus never took his eyes off him. When the man came with the sugar, Seamus barked the price. I don't know the cost of things, unless it's drink, which always costs more than I can ever afford and not just financially.

But even I knew this was through the roof. I was going to ask,

"What? The Budget came early?"

I doubt he'd have heard me, so intent was he on the man. After he'd gone, Seamus said,

"Bloody thieves."

"You know him?"

"No, never saw him before."

"Then how . . . ?"

He glared at me, venom jumping in his eyes, said,

"They're all thieves and liars, and God knows what diseases they bring in."

I was too stunned to reply. His eyes cleared and he switched to friendly mode, asked,

"So, what can I do you for, Jack?"

I bought a box of Black Magic and a birthday card. He told me a joke that involved a priest and Irish stew. Thank God, I have no recollection of it. It was lewd and certainly not funny; he enjoyed it immensely. I do remember him calling as I left,

"Don't be a stranger, hear?"

"We are the graceless and dumbfounded, insane with our own insatiable desire for another time and place."

David Means, *Assorted Fire Events*

The rain came hammering down. One of those showers that seems personal, as if it really wants to drench you.

It did.

I remember what Billy Connolly said, that there isn't bad weather, only wrong clothes. Give him six months in Galway, see what he'd say then. I got on the bus and barely found a seat, it was so crowded. Sat by a window and tried to figure what was different. Irish. Everybody was speaking it. I heard a flurry of,

"An bhfuil tú go maith?"

"Cén chaoi bhfuil tú?"

"Tá an aimsir go dona."

My favourite was from a young man who answered one of the above with,

"Tá scéilín agam."

He'd a story to tell. The translation doesn't do justice to the emphasis he laid on *"scéilín."* Combining intrigue, pleasure, excitement and the low cunning of renown. I'd like to have heard that story. Just before the bus moved off, a young girl, late teens, rushed on board wearing a sky blue windbreaker. Looked round at the full bus, asked me,

"Is that seat, like, taken?"

American.

I smiled, said,

"Work away."

She sat, went,

"I love the way you guys talk."

As the bus pulled off, from old habit, I blessed myself and she was thrilled, said,

"Gee, that is, like, so cute."

I didn't have a reply to this. She continued to stare at me. I noticed a ring in her left eyebrow and a stud beneath her lower lip. That shit has got to hurt.

To break the stare, I asked,

"Are you on holidays?"

"That's like vacation, right? Yeah, you could say that, but it's, like, a drag, you hear what I'm saying?"

"Why?"

She rolled her eyes and I sensed it was her party piece, something she did a lot. She answered,

"My dad, he's like this old guy, fifty-two, and he wants me to learn about my roots. Like, hello?"

I like Americans, their vitality amazes me, and the fresh energy they carry, it's downright mysterious. Me, I was born tired. I decided to make the effort, asked,

"Your father's people are from Connemara?"

"Yeah, right, like he doesn't mention it a zillion times. So, I'm staying with his sister and she's so, like . . . anxious. Like, worries all the time. She needs, like, you know, to chill."

It wasn't the easiest thing to follow her speech; if she said "like" one more time, I'd scream. I asked,

"What does she worry about?"

"Like stuff, you know?"

That was all the insight she had. We were coming into Salthill and I wanted to watch the bay. Lest she mar the pleasure of it, I asked,

"How do you fill your time?"

"Fill?"

"What do you do all day?"

"Oh, I got you. Mostly I hang . . . like, around the mall, watch the guys."

Mall!

I was still keeping one eye on the bay, waves crashing in over the rocks, went,

"You enjoy that?"

"It sucks."

I spotted the hotel and moved to signal the driver. The girl asked,

"What's the deal with the stick?"

"I hurt my knee."

"Bummer."

I wasn't heartbroken to be leaving her but tried,

"Take care."

"Yeah. Like, whatever."

When I got off the bus, the wind nearly blew me over. The girl was staring out the window, so I gave what I thought was a friendly wave. She gave me the finger.

The Connemara Coast Hotel looks like a motel, long and sleek and strung out along the very edge of the land. I got inside and felt grateful for the warmth. Located the lounge, and there were Ridge and Margaret. I approached and said,

"Happy birthday."

Ridge grimaced, said to Margaret,

"This is him."

Not the most effusive welcome. Margaret put out her hand, said,

"I'm Margaret, nice to meet you."

I don't know what I'd expected. A bull dyke if I was honest. She was in her late forties, with ash blond hair, cut in a pageboy. Brown wide eyes, a too large nose and great mouth: those lips that you want to reach out and touch. Dressed in a black polo and jeans, her body seemed strong, in shape. I was conscious of my cane, my age, and straightened my back. Ridge, observing me, smiled. Margaret said,

"You look frozen. Will you have a drink?"

And got the look from Ridge. I knew she'd cautioned Margaret about the alky, who had the grace to look confused, so I said,

"Some coffee would be good."

She rose, headed off. I said to Ridge,

"She's not what I expected."

This amused her and she asked,

"What were you expecting?"

How to answer that? I tried a half truth, said,

"Hostility."

"It's early yet."

Margaret returned with a tray, bearing sandwiches and a pot of coffee, said,

"Milk."

And went off again. I surveyed the tray and said,

"I'm warming to her already."

Then it struck Ridge, awareness travelling from her eyes to light up a wicked smile. She clapped her hands, exclaimed,

"I don't believe it."

I had no idea what she was on about, said,

"I've no idea what you're on about."

"Margaret, oh my God, you thought she was gay. That's priceless."

I felt my heart soar even as I kicked myself for presumption, went,

"She's not gay?"

Ridge was shaking her head, said,

"God, I should have known, you are some kind of di-nosaur."

Margaret returned with the milk, looked at us, asked,

"Did I miss something?"

Ridge sat back, said,

"Not a lot."

To move on, I produced the Black Magic and card. Margaret smiled and Ridge actually was surprised. She took the card, said,

"I guess you bought this in a hurry."

And slid the card over. On the front was,

"Dad, on your birthday."

I had no reply. I wasn't going to relate the story about the non-national and the sugar. They'd have said I should have walked out. Ridge began to open the chocolates, said,

"Thanks for the thought."

She offered the box. I declined but Margaret took two.

The urge to say "fuckit", march to the bar and get hammered was powerful. Margaret poured coffee for me, and for a moment there was an awkward silence. Then Margaret asked Ridge,

"What time are your parents coming?"

I was surprised, had always thought of Ridge as being alone. Placing her in a family setting didn't seem to gel. You asked yourself, "What is wrong with this picture?" There was something in Ridge, like myself, that set the seal of solitary around her. She answered,

"They should be here any minute. Can you wait?"

Margaret checked her watch, said,

"I'd love to but I've got an early shift."

She stood up, leaned over and kissed Ridge on the cheek, asked me,

"Would you like a lift, Jack?"

"You're going into town?"

"Yes."

I looked at Ridge, who rooted in her bag, passed over the book, said,

"Take the lift."

I didn't look at the volume, just put it in my pocket. Margaret had a drink in front of her but hadn't touched it and I asked,

"What about your drink?"

"I had one already. With all you guards around, I have to be careful."

I let that go and said to Ridge,

"I'll call you."

"Do."

It wasn't a request; it was an order.

Margaret had a light blue Escort that looked new. She got behind the wheel and I sat beside her, fastening the seat belt. Took me a time as my cane kept getting entangled. She said,

"Let me help you."

As she leaned over, I could smell her perfume. It certainly wasn't any relation of the Woolworth's special. I felt a stir of desire. God knows, I couldn't recall the last time that happened. Then she smiled and put the car in gear. She drove well, capable and assured. I asked,

"Do you work?"

She gave a surprised laugh, said,

"Of course I work, what do you think? I'm a nurse."

"Where?"

She shot a look, asked,

"Is this an interrogation?"

"Sorry, I was curious."

She didn't answer for a moment. We'd come along the top of the golf course, reaching Taylor's Hill. She asked then,

"Do you have ten minutes?"

"Sure."

"I like to park on the prom when it's wild, like now. The sight of the bay, it's wonderful. Would that be OK?"

When I nodded, she said,

"I'm a nurse at the Bon Secours, used to be called Galvia."

I couldn't resist, said,

"Nursing for the rich."

She didn't like it and had heard it before, countered,

"They don't deserve treatment?"

Her tone riled me and I countered,

"Sure they do, they just don't deserve special treatment."

She was parking the car, with great skill. I imagined she'd do most things well. The sea was indeed spectacular, the waves crashing against the diving boards of Blackrock. It roused a sense of recklessness in my soul. I wanted to get back out on the edge of existence, to have the adrenalin roar in my blood. I could almost taste the madness in my mouth, realised Margaret was talking and said,

"Sorry, what?"

"Bríd says you're attempting to change your life."

"Bríd has a big mouth."

That didn't go down too good and she followed,

"She thinks you'll fail, that you'll drink again as you always do."

I opened the door and with difficulty got out, said,

"Think I'll walk."

She was trying to apologise, but I slammed the door, the wind emphasising the aggressiveness of the gesture. As I turned into the fierce weather, I nearly lost my cane and wanted to sling it out into the bay. Before I could button my coat, I was completely soaked.

"He wondered if the problem of evil enhanced as time moved on and new evil was added to old or whether each new evil brought the world closer to the end of evil."

Sean Burke, *Deadwater*

When I got back to Bailey's, I was wet from head to toe. Tore my clothes off and climbed into the shower. Finally got some heat into my bones, put on a faded sweatshirt and got the book from my jacket. It was another book of plays by Synge,

The Playboy of the Western World and Other Plays.

I took a deep breath, opened the cover, and there it was, in large black writing:

THE DRAMATIST

I flipped through the pages, and one piece was high-lighted in red marker. I decided to try and memorise that, instinct telling me it was a component in the puzzle.

It's you three will not see age or death coming; you that were my company when the fires on the hilltops were put out and the stars were our friends only. I'll turn my thoughts back from

this night—that's pitiful for want of pity—to the time it was your rods and cloaks made a little tent for me where there'd be a birch tree making shelter, and on a dry stone; though from this day my own fingers will be making a tent for me, spreading out my hairs and they knotted with the rain.

Now I knew. Two girls had been killed, apparently accidentally. A book by Synge beneath each of them with the words "The Dramatist" written inside. So what did I do and who was going to believe me? Moved to the back page and, sure enough, typed on a label and pasted in there was "Deirdre, demented under the burden of her sorrow, falls lifeless across the open grave". At least I could confirm the suspicions of Stewart the drug dealer. Tell him he was right: someone had killed his sister. I had absolutely nothing to go on. Even if I did, what the hell was I going to do, pursue the killer? The phone went and I picked up, heard,

"Jack?"

It was Jeff and his voice was heavy. He said,

"Pat Young is in hospital."

"What happened to him?"

"He was attacked."

"By who?"

He took a moment and I knew he was selecting his words carefully, then,

"The current terminology is, I believe, by person or persons unknown."

The sarcasm dripped from the phone. I'd known Jeff in

most moods, seen him grope through pain, despair, but never, never had he used this pitch and especially not with me. I tried to move away from that, asked,

"Is he badly hurt?"

"Depends on how you define badly."

My anger flashed but I kept my tone level, asked,

"Is he conscious?"

"Luckily, no."

Now I was unable to rein it in, said,

"Are we going to dance around much longer? What do I have to do, take three guesses?"

"Gee, Jack, you sound worked up. I didn't think you cared that much what happened to Pat?"

I let that go, probably because it was true. If I let rip— and every fibre of my being urged me to—our friendship might not recover. My mouth had been the cause of numerous disasters, so for once I didn't get into the ring. I waited, then asked,

"Is he going to make it?"

"I hope not."

Took me blindside and I was unable to proceed. He said,

"If you were castrated, would you want to *make it*?"

The end words were spat, the venom in full flight. I said, "Jesus."

"I don't think He had much to do with it."

"Who did?"

Now his voice was winding down and a deep fatigue moving in. He said,

"I already told you; actually I told you twice."

What had he told me? I'd no idea, asked,

"What did you tell me?"

He let out a long suppressed breath, said,

"You weren't listening. Like Cathy says, you never do."

Click.

I held the phone in my hand, the dial tone mocking me. I wanted to go down to Nestor's, confront him and find out what the hell he was talking about. But I hadn't the energy. Got into bed and felt as bad as I ever did. Expected to spend the night tossing and turning. Sleep came fast and deep. The dreams were vivid.

My mother, in an open grave, shouting, *"Jack, I can't move. Help me."* I had a shovel in my hand and began to pile in the clay. Jeff, holding a copy of Synge's book, whispering *"Why don't you listen?"* and then tossing the book. As is the way with dreams, logic wasn't evident. The book landed beside the grave and I screamed, *"I can't bury that. I don't understand what's happening."* Then I was limping along the coast road, without my cane. Margaret and Ridge were further along, taunting, *"Hey, catch up."*

I couldn't.

When I woke in the morning, the bed seemed like a bomb had hit it. I was covered in sweat. I was experiencing what they term an emotional hangover. Nearly as bad as the real thing. Dragged myself to the bathroom, risked a look in the mirror.

Jesus.

How old was I getting? Could definitely see new lines on my face, deep imbedded ones. Took a long scalding shower and was clean if nothing else. Over coffee, I resolved to start tracking "The Dramatist". Dressed to detect, in faded cords, sweatshirt and my guard's coat. As I left the room, I wish I could say I was filled with zeal or a sense of purpose. No, I was tired. Mrs Bailey, peering intently at the *Irish Independent,* said,

"Guards, guards, guards."

"What?"

"In Donegal, there's a fierce scandal about bribery, intimidation, cover-ups, and in Dublin seventeen guards have been suspended after that public demonstration. In my day, a guard might turn a blind eye to poteen, but now they've lost the run of themselves."

A whole lost era in that expression "to lose the run of yourself". It's a desperate crime in the Irish catalogue, to have ideas above your station, believing yourself above the common herd. It's akin to having "notions", and that is the bottom rung on the vanity ladder. My own battered history with the guards makes me an unlikely advocate on their behalf. I said,

"They're all we've got."

She actually blessed herself . . . "In the name of the Father . . ." Then added,

"God help us all."

That ended the case for the defence. I left her to the paper and the state of the country, walked down to the Augustinian church and considered lighting some candles. The amount of people needing help would require more candles than I could light. I passed by. Next to the church is a French restaurant, then a steep flight of stone steps, followed by a store front. I moved to the right of the steps, tried to visualise how the student had fallen. No doubt that a fall from them could kill you. Across the street is a small outlet that sells silver jewellery. Seems to do a brisk trade. A woman came out, watched me, and I gave a noncommittal wave. That seemed to decide her and she crossed over.

She had a gypsy look, dark hair to her shoulders, dark eyes, sallow complexion. Wearing one of those long billowing skirts that suit nobody. They proclaim, "I've lousy legs." I'd have put her age at forty, but lines around her eyes, the side of her mouth—maybe older. What she most definitely was, was attractive. A grace in her movements. She said,

"*Quel dommage*, what a pity."

French? . . . or affected?

I asked,

"Did you know the girl?"

"Yes, she had a small apartment at the top of the steps."

I looked again, went,

"People live up there?"

"She did. In the city now there are apartments in the most unlikely places."

Her English was perfect but with a slight overlay of accent. Also a trace of an Irish tone that people acquire who learn English in Ireland. A softening of the vowels and the barest hint of a lilt. I decided to plead ignorance, see what she'd tell, said,

"I don't really know what happened."

She seemed happy to oblige, said,

"Karen, Karen Lowe, she'd have been living there about a year, often popped into the shop. The night it happened, she'd been out with some friends and left them around ten. At 10:45 p.m. someone saw her lying there, called the ambulance and the guards."

I tried to frame the next question as delicately as possible, asked,

"Could she have been drinking?"

Vehement shake of the head.

"No, I know her . . . oh, *mon dieu* . . . knew her. She'd go to the pub but never more than a glass of shandy."

Then she stared at me, said,

"You're not the police?"

"No, no, . . . I'm a . . . from the insurance company."

She near spat, said,

"*Merde!* They like to make the people pay the money but to pay back . . . never. You know how much my premium is for the shop?"

I didn't want to carry the can for an insurance company but had to venture,

"A lot?"

Her head was nodding furiously, a trace of spittle at the

corner of her mouth. I reassessed my original opinion as to her being attractive. I now had her pegged as demented. She said,

"You tell them cocksuckers . . ."

Pause.

She looked at me, asked,

"Is that the correct word?"

Who was I to argue? It was not the description I'd have expected from a French lady. I'd have thought something classier, insulting but elegant, as is their birthright. But my turn to nod, if less energetically, and she continued,

"You tell them to pay up."

"I will."

And I moved away. For a brief moment I'd been thinking I'd ask her out; now I thought she needed locking up. When I got to the Oxfam shop, I risked looking back. She was still there, hands on hips, seething. I turned right and headed for the Eyre Square Centre. I wondered was this "the mall" my American teenager frequented? On the ground floor, there's an open plan café. I went to the counter, got an espresso, saw the young blond guy who'd been tailing me. He waved, indicated a free table and sat down.

I paid for the coffee and the girl said,

"Have a lovely day."

It threw me and I grumbled some vague reply. It's not easy to carry a cup when you have a cane and it took me a time to reach the table.

The blond guy stood up, said,

"Let me help."

Took the coffee, set it down then settled himself. He was younger close up, no more than eighteen. I sat down and looked him full in the face. His left eye, there was something off about it. He smiled, said,

"Jack Taylor."

As if we were old friends. I launched,

"Who the hell are you?"

His smile faded, consternation on his face, as if he couldn't believe I didn't know. He asked,

"You don't remember me?"

"No, I don't."

With a frown between his eyes, highlighting the oddness of the left, his act was heavily dependent on my knowing who he was. He said with a hint of desperation,

"I'm Ronan Wall."

I took out my cigs, did it slowly, a whole ceremony of rooting for my lighter. Impatience was coursing through him, and when I eventually lit up and exhaled, I said,

"You say that like it should mean something. It don't mean shit to me, pal."

The "pal" was not received well. His fingers were tapping on the table and he reluctantly said,

"The swans."

Now I remembered. A few years back, swans were being decapitated in the Claddagh Basin. The Swan Society had hired me to investigate. Not the best period of my life. I

was deeply immersed in very heavy events, and it took me
a while to focus. It meant nights huddled against a wall,
fending off the swans and inner demons. I did catch the
culprit, a sixteen-year-old who was seriously deranged.
He'd lost an eye as a result. I recalled he came from a priv-
ileged background and the whole affair was thus hushed
up. Apart from the eye, he bore no resemblance to the lu-
natic I'd encountered then. I said,

"You've changed."

Now, he was back in the game. He sat up straight, answered,

"Completely."

A smugness had entered his voice, the tone of someone
who has reached the heights, no longer susceptible to petty
weaknesses. I stubbed out the cigarette, looked full into his
face, said,

"I meant physically."

He pulled back, hesitated, then,

"I'm cured."

I could play, went,

"That's great. No desire to massacre swans any more?"

I saw his fists clench. The recent jauntiness was slipping
and he tried a smile, said,

"I wasn't well then but I got help, the best available,
and . . . I'm a student now, getting A's."

I felt an instinctive dislike for this kid. That's all he was,
but something older, malignant, was all around him. I
asked,

"What are you studying? I doubt you're planning on being a vet, or have you changed—sorry, been cured—to that extent?"

He was with the game now; his eyes, or eye, took a more intense focus. A smile at the corner of his mouth, he said,

"I'm doing an arts degree."

Numbers clicked in my head and my mind joined the dots, raced to a mad conclusion. He'd been stalking me, had a history of violence, and now here he was, presenting what? I took a breath, asked,

"Any Synge required?"

"What?"

"John Millington Synge. Come on, you're studying literature, any *dramatist* on there?"

If he was guilty, he wasn't showing it. I had to tread carefully. The last time I named a killer, I was wrong and an innocent young man had been slaughtered. The reverberations of that horrendous mistake would haunt my days. I couldn't possibly afford to go down that road again. I went the simple route, asked,

"Why are you following me?"

Now he was animated, as if he thought I'd never ask, answered,

"I wanted to thank you."

"You what?"

"Honestly, I was very ill, headed down a road of serious trouble, but you came along, and as a result, I got help and here I am, a whole new person."

There was a mocking edge to his voice, so I said,

"Let me see if I got this straight, I hit you with a stun gun, you went in the water, the swans went at your face and you lost an eye. For that, you want to thank me?"

The recapping of the events had a strange effect. His face seemed to light up, as if the narration had got his juices going. He said,

"Can I shake your hand, Jack?"

The last thing I wanted to do was touch this guy. I went, "What you could do, you could help me out."

Suspicion and malevolence danced across his face. He said,

"You name it, big guy."

I told him about the two dead students, that I was investigating for the insurance companies. Could he ask around, seeing he was on campus, find out about their friends and any relevant information? He reached in his pocket, took out a spiral notebook, pen, asked for their names and details. I said I'd pay him for his time. He shrugged that off; money was not a problem. I asked for his phone number and he handed me a card, saw my astonishment, said,

"I'm a very organised person. You want to give me yours?"

"Mine?"

"Yes, your business card. Does it say *'Private Investigator, Discretion Guaranteed'*?"

Now he was fucking with me. I said I didn't have one and he nodded, as if he understood. I said,

"You've been tracking me so you already know where I live."

I stood up, got a grip on my cane and he stared, fascinated. For a moment, I wondered what he was seeing? Then he jerked back from the momentary lapse, asked,

"What happened?"

"A hurling accident."

I walked away and he shouted,

"We're alike, you know."

I didn't look back, said,

"I don't think so."

But he had the final word with,

"We're both injured but moving on—moving on and up."

Put music to it, you had the making of a country song.

"There are sides of all that western life, the groggy-patriot-publican-general-shop-man who is married to the priest's half sister and is second cousin once-removed of the dispensary doctor, that are horrible and awful. This is the type that is running the present United Irish League anti-grazier campaign, while they're swindling the people themselves in a dozen ways and then buying out their holdings and packing whole families off to America."

J.M. Synge in a letter to Stephen McKenna

For the next few weeks, I gathered information on the dead stu-dents. Talked to their friends, classmates, and turned up nothing. Mentioned Synge to them and drew blank faces. Ronan Wall, the swan guy, rang me often and offered no clue as to how I should proceed. If he was the Dramatist, I had no way of proving it. His tone continued to be a mix of baiting, flattery and arrogance. He even said,

"Who'd have expected us to become friends?"

I couldn't let that go, asked,

"You think we're friends?"

"Oh yeah, Jack, we're close."

I called Ridge and she said there was no evidence of foul play. When I mentioned the book, she said she couldn't explain that. Perhaps it was a bizarre coincidence, one of those thousand-to-one chances that defy logic. I'd lost patience, asked,

"You really believe that?"

"Does it matter? We have nothing else, or rather you have nothing else."

"There's somebody out there, playing a weird game and getting away with murder."

Changing the subject, she said,

"Write down this number."

I got a pen and she read the digits. I wrote them down, asked,

"And I'm going to do what with this number?"

Her exasperation was audible and she answered,

"If you're smart, you'll call. It's Margaret."

"Margaret?"

"Yes, I'm as surprised as you sound. What on earth she sees in you is beyond comprehension. I gather your previous encounter wasn't exactly promising."

My heartbeat had increased, a wave of near delight swept through me, yet I couldn't believe what I was hearing. Ridge's obvious displeasure didn't help. I asked

"She's interested in me?"

Her derision was clear and she snapped,

"Did I say she was interested? Did you hear me say that? Your ability to jump to conclusions is beyond belief. I said to call her, but if you mess her around, you'll answer to me."

"Jeez, Ridge, that sounds like a threat."

"It is."

Click.

I did call Margaret and she responded with warmth and, Good Lord, affection. As a young man, I hadn't been what you could ever term a ladies' man. Alcoholics have a deadly combination of ego and no self-esteem. It sure confuses the hell out of you. You select a woman who is top of your wish list (ego dictates this), then the lack of self-esteem dismantles every single reason she might ever consider you. So, you move way down the scale and search out the grateful ones. Their gratitude lies in that hardly anyone would ever consider them. Thus the dual damage, the hurt, has piled on already. The whole shabby ritual is pre-ordained to failure. The guys you know, they sneer,

"She's a nice girl."

In macho terms, she doesn't, as the Americans say, "put out". In other words, buddy, you ain't getting any. But you go with the flow. Drink conceals the flaws and cracks in such endeavours. Back then, you "did a line". No, not cocaine. This was before we learned about relationships. You followed the strict ritual: brought her to the pictures, then progressed to an evening's restrained drinking. She'd have an orange or, wow, if she was forward, a Babycham. While at the bar, you hammered in some serious short ones, then took a pint back to sit with her and sip. Moved on to going dancing on Saturday night, the showbands in their heyday. Here the nightmare began in earnest. My generation didn't dance. The girls could jive and move till the cows came home. The guys poured the booze from prohibited flasks, did the "slow set" and got to lay a hand on her shoulder, perhaps feel the bra strap and be hot for weeks. If you were coerced into joining her for the fast numbers, you demonstrated how child of the sixties you were. Did a series of quirky disjointed twitches without moving your feet and sweated ferociously. It bore an uncanny resemblance to the DTs and may have been the very early rehearsal. Not till Ann Henderson did I ever fall in love. And I blew that to smithereens.

So Margaret and I began to do a millennium version of "the line" of that forgotten era. We went to the cinema, took short walks to the Claddagh and fed the swans.

Galway stuff.

I didn't tell her about the swan killer. Once, near the church, I saw him leaning against the statue of the Blessed Virgin. And I mean leaning, his shoulder against hers, his legs loose as if he was her buddy. A time there was, the priest would have been out, clipping him around the ear, going,

"Yah impertinent pup, who's your father?"

Not any more. Priests were so gun-shy they had to keep the profile lower than a wet Monday novena. With the deluge of scandals, the clergy no longer expected the respect of the people; they simply wanted to avoid lynch mobs.

Ronan, of course, waved and Margaret asked,

"You know him?"

How to answer that? I said,

"We've met."

She stared at him, said,

"He's leaning against Our Lady."

"He sure is."

His body shifted and his right arm circled the waist of the statue. Margaret was infuriated, went,

"Somebody should speak to him."

The plea of our times. As public disorder increases and hooligans become more blatant, the plea goes unheeded. I said, as many do,

"Forget it."

And we walked on, contributing our own tiny morsel to the vast sea of shirked responsibility that eats at the fabric of decency.

Margaret was forty-five and had been briefly married, to "a cold man". Her exact words. After two years of ice, she got a separation. I said,

"You're technically still married?"

She gave a sad smile and an answer that captures the essence of the Irish woman.

"If marriage is about love, then we were never married."

And didn't mention him again. How interested was I anyway? I told her of my own disastrous union to Kiki, and I'd even less to say than she did. So we left the marriages in our wake, trailing sadness. I took her to see a John B. Keane play at the Town Hall which she loved. My mind was on Synge and how little of his work I knew. I resolved to get down to Charlie Byrne's, remedy that.

Bed.

We circled round that issue, wary and apprehensive. I kissed her goodnight a few times and felt her grip me a little more tightly each time. I'd been to her home, a spacious top floor flat in Greenfields. She'd even cooked me dinner, Irish stew, saying,

"I have you down as the meat and potatoes type."

I didn't protest.

The only item missing on our programme of dating was the pub, the very basis of most Irish courtship. I figured I'd better deal with that, said,

"We can go for a drink. I won't be suffering."

She gave me a long look, then,

"I'm not a big drinker, some wine with meals, but it's not a vital part of my life."

I never did get to see her have that infrequent glass but didn't push it. She did ask,

"Are you afraid of physical intimacy?"

Which is down to the wire. No evasive hints there. I said,

"No, I'm a bit beat up. When I get back to speed, I'm planning on making a move."

Got an enigmatic smile and she said,

"Let's get you on that road to recovery."

She had a friend, a physiotherapist, who agreed to treat me. I began a punishing regime with her and was soon able to discard the cane. My knee was never going to be 100 per cent, but it sure was coming along. The day I ditched the cane, I made love to Margaret. A Friday night. We'd been for a meal, went back to her place, and I made the promised move. It wasn't a huge success; in fact it was mostly quick. We lay in bed after and I said,

"I'll improve."

She had her head on my shoulder, answered,

"You better."

War with Iraq dominated the news and people became familiar with UN resolutions. Hans Blix was as famous as Bono. The pool run by the sentry in Nestor's, as to when Bush would invade, had been abandoned. I asked him,

"What happens to all the money in the pot?"

He was staring into his Guinness, snapped,

"All bets are off."

Pithy. Put it on a tombstone and you were downright ironic. Refunds weren't mentioned.

The rupture in my friendship with Jeff began to mend and I resumed my visits. The hard chair and table that served as my office were back in action. I heard that Pat, Jeff's friend who'd been castrated, had been moved to Dublin to be treated there. Sometimes, his fate shadowed our conversations, but we never met it head on.

To my surprise, Cathy asked me to mind their toddler, Serena May. I went,

"Like babysit?"

"Exactly."

"Jeez, Cathy, I don't know."

Cathy had put on weight and it suited her. She'd taken on the role of mother, housewife, with delight. A far cry from the heroin punk I'd originally known. Almost all traces of her London accent were gone. I felt that was a loss. She spoke like an actress who'd determined to pass as Irish. Mostly, she succeeded.

The afternoons and evenings I watched Serena, I felt a kind of tranquillity. The little girl wasn't walking but she sure could move on all fours. She seemed to know me and sat still as a prayer when I read to her. Dr Seuss, Barney and a shitpile of nursery rhymes. I also read to her in Irish, and if Cathy returned early, she'd say,

"Don't stop. I love to hear that language."

Usually, *M'Asal Beag Dubh. The Little Black Donkey* by Pádraic Ó Conaire. I didn't remark to Cathy that here was a drunk, reading from a drunk. She said,

"I hear you're seeing someone."

Galway, city or no, it was still a small town. I muttered,

"Yes, sort of . . ."

She laughed, demanded,

"When will we meet her?"

"Soon, real soon."

An event was coming down the pike, already shaping in its black destructive energy and preparing to rip my life in pieces, pieces that would never be restored. Cathy said,

"You're doing good."

And like a fool, I answered,

"Better than I ever could have hoped."

"Not that it matters, but I tried to think of a way to repay your generosity; and such repayment invariably settled on the truth that you'd be better rid of me. Be happy and tell my sons that I was a drunk, a dreamer, a weakling and a madman, anything but that I did not love them."

Frederick Exley, *A Fan's Notes*

Christmas came and went and I stayed sober. By New Year, I was off the cigarettes. Twice a week, I went to visit my mother and swore I'd get her moved.

I didn't.

She had shifted to another place in her head, a place where she was a young girl again and I'd no idea what she was talking about. My relationship with the matron continued to be cold and combative. My investigation into the students' deaths came to a complete stop. I spoke to Stewart on the phone, told him I was getting nowhere. He said,

"Keep searching."

And hung up.

The cheques continued to arrive and I continued to cash them. Ronan Wall rang me less and less often, his interest in play waning. Margaret and I were still "doing our line" and my life was as normal as it gets. My knee had improved but a slight limp was going to last.

I was in Charlie Byrne's, looking for books on Synge, collared Vinny, asked him if he could help. Much as he hates to admit defeat, he conceded that Synge was not one of his areas of expertise, but added,

"Here's the man you want."

I turned to see a distinguished man, standing next to the literary criticism. Vinny said,

"My old professor of English and a published author."

He added quickly,

"Not that he's old, but college was a time ago. He's the Synge expert."

The man smiled politely; he had an air of academia. There was that awkward moment when strangers have been introduced and have nothing to say. I muttered,

"I'm looking to find out a little about Synge."

He gave a tolerant smile, the one that says, we both know you're an idiot. He said,

"Read his account of his time on the Aran islands."

I said I would and then, after another anxious minute, he said goodbye and moved away.

Vinny provided the following:

Interpreting Synge, Essays from the Synge Summer School, 1991–2000, edited by Nicholas Grene.

An Aran Reader, edited by Breandán and Ruairi Ó hEithir.

An Aran Keening by Andrew McNcillie.

Scenes of Aran Pilgrimage by Tim Robinson.

As he wrapped them, I said,

"Take me a while to wade through these."

"But you'll know the man."

"You sure?"

"Sure as shooting."

A few days later, as I walked into the hotel, Mrs Bailey said,

"Mr Taylor, a letter for you."

She never would, despite my pleas, call me Jack. I took the letter, a plain white envelope. Typed on the front was:

Jack Taylor
Bailey's Hotel
Galway

I shoved it in my pocket and took the stairs to my room. A wreath was lying against my door. Yes, the ones you see on top of coffins. I picked it up, a chill along my spine. God, I needed a cigarette. Put my hand down to reach for them and remembered, no cigs. Opened my door, went in, stood lost for a moment, then moved to the window, pulled it up and flung the wreath into the yard. My mind was racing through answers. A practical joke? A mistake? But none brought ease. I sat on the bed and longed for the days I could have reached for the bottle of Jameson, drunk deep from the neck.

Took the envelope out of my pocket, saw the tremble in my hand, then tore the flap and took out a mass card. The Sacred Heart on the front, inside the words,

"A mass will be offered for the repose of the soul of Jack Taylor."

Then,

"With deepest sympathy from"

In bold black letters:

J.M. SYNGE

My breathing was constricted and I thought I was going to throw up. It passed and I looked at the envelope. It had been posted in Galway the previous evening. The wreath he'd delivered personally, but a hotel has people in and out all day.

I picked up the phone and rang Ridge, told her. She was quiet as she digested this, then,

"Somebody's playing with you."

"Oh really, wow, I'm glad I cleared that up. Lucky I called you."

"Don't use that tone with me, Jack Taylor."

I backed off, tried,

"Well, at least now you'll agree he's out there, that it wasn't, what did you call it . . . a bizarre coincidence?"

She sighed, asked,

"So what? It doesn't really change anything. I mean, what can you do?"

"Do? I can watch my frigging back."

And I slammed down the phone.

A line of coke, a carton of cigs, a bottle of Jameson, nineteen pints of Guinness, all preened, shimmered before my eyes. I got out of the room and asked Mrs Bailey if she'd noticed anything, anyone odd passing through the lobby. She looked at me in disbelief.

"Odd? Are you codding me? The whole country's odd. A young lad was in this morning, looking for work, and he had pins in his eyebrows, his tongue and the Lord only knows where else."

I wanted escape, to shut off my mind. Went to the video store and rented a whole set of stuff. The guy said,

"Catching up?"

"As if I could."

Over the next few days, I saw *Insomnia, The Devil's Backbone, Lantana, Donnie Darko, Three Colours Blue, Apocalypse Redux* and the whole of the first series of *CSI*.

Maybe I'd watched *The Simpsons* too often, but I punctuated the movies with Domino's pizza, delivered regularly. Finally, my mind was sufficiently bombarded to get back on track. Rang Margaret and took a walk along the prom. Late February, the wind howling off the bay, sure it was cold but invigorating. Then headed for the Galleon, our appetites up. Margaret ordered Chicken Maryland and "loads of chips", asked,

"Jack?"

I studied the menu, said,

"Well, it's not going to be pizza."

"I thought you loved it?"

"Not any more."

I ordered steak, roast potatoes. Margaret's face was flush from the wind, her eyes alive with contentment. I said,

"You look like you've had good news."

Huge smile and,

"I have, I have. I didn't want to tell you till it was con-firmed, but I've got a place for your mother in Castlegar."

"Castlegar?"

"It's a wonderful nursing home with a long waiting list. The care is the very best and it has a fantastic reputation."

I didn't know how to reply and she frowned, asked,

"Did I do wrong? Was I too presumptuous? It's just I know how worried you've been."

I reached over, took her hand, said,

"I'm delighted. I've felt so guilty, so ashamed of leaving her in that kip. Thank you from the bottom of my heart."

She was all lit up, said,

"You can have your mother transferred immediately."

"I'll do it tomorrow."

Back at her home, I made love as if I meant it. She said, "That was wonderful."

Which is pushing it, but it was a whole lot better. Margaret had an early shift at the hospital, so I slipped out of there just before 1 a.m. She was already asleep, and I touched her face with my fingertips, tracing the line of her jaw. Even in sleep, you could see the strength she possessed.

Outside, a cab passed but I felt too good, decided to relish the walk. A sense of well-being coursed through me and I wanted to savour it. Coming up on Newcastle, I vaguely registered a black van parked ahead. As I drew level the door slid open, and before I could look, I got a crack to the side of my head.

Blackness.

When I came to, the first realisation was the intense pain behind my eyes. I was sitting in a hard chair but not restrained. I was in some type of basement, seated at the end of a long wooden table. Turned my head. Christ, it hurt. Two men in black hoods were behind me. I faced front and saw a man at the opposite end, also seated. Two men behind him, like we were playing poor man's chess. All were hooded, with holes for eyes, nose, mouth. Their clothing was dark, casual, but suggested a military slant.

The seated man had a bulky upper body, thick wrists, stubby fingers. His hands were joined loosely, relaxed. He said,

"Ah, Jack, let me apologise to you for the manner of your transportation. The blow to your head was professionally administered. You'll have an ache but nothing serious."

I found my voice, said,

"That's a fucking relief."

He smiled, smoker's teeth against the hood. I saw two long metal poles behind the standing men, crisscrossed like an emblem. He followed my look, said,

"Pikes."

I brought my eyes back to him, asked,

"What are ye, paramilitaries?"

He laughed, turned for a moment as if to share the joke with his men, said,

"No, but we are fighting a war."

I remembered Jeff's friend, Pat, suspected of molesting the young girl, arrested, released, then savagely mutilated. I said,

"The Pikemen . . . Jesus, you're the crowd who near killed Pat Young."

He nodded, as if bowing to an achievement, and that infuriated me. My voice rose, went,

"Fucking vigilantes."

And got a crack to the side of the head. He said,

"No obscenities, Jack. If we are to stem the tide of decay, we must apply standards in every sphere of our lives."

I massaged my head, said,

"And you'll set the standards, that it?"

The nicotine-stained smile again, then he stood, moved to the metal poles, said,

"Behold the formidable pike. In 1798, during the rebellion, they were easier to use than a musket or bayonet."

A note of pride and admiration had entered his voice. He continued,

"Pikes were the principal weapon used by the rebels—very effective for the close-in stuff, the man-to-man combat. The original pike was six inches long and spear-shaped. The handle, originally, was about six feet, but we've allowed ourselves a little leverage."

I gave a short laugh now, said,

"It's not all you've allowed yourselves."

Anger sparked in his eyes, and I could gather he didn't like interruption. Here was a guy accustomed to lecturing while others listened. He gave a brief cough and I could hear the wheezing in his chest; he'd been, or still was, a heavy smoker.

VICIOUS CIRCLE

"He likes a drink
And that's to understate
What is, in fact
The whole of life for him."

Gerard Hanberry: from *Rough Night*

The guy moved to the wall, tenderly took down one of the pikes, ran his fingers along the top, said,

"Later on, a hook was added to the side of the pike head. Apart from anything else, it could be used to sever the reins of the horses to dismount the rider."

He droned on about the lethal beauty of the weapon, its ferocious simplicity. I felt the guys behind me shuffle their feet. They'd heard this before. Their shoes, I looked at them, raised my head, said,

"These guys, they're guards."

He raised the pike above his head, shouted,

"We are the new guards."

And slammed the pike into the centre of the wood table, the head imbedded a good three inches. The handle quivered with the force. Yeah, it got me and my body gave a jump. I felt anger build, asked,

"That what you used on the poor bastard, to disembowel him? How many of ye to hold him down?"

He gave the smile again,

"We've been watching you, Jack. In your own small way, you too have been fighting the evil that goes unpunished. You were a guard, too. Join us."

I was lost for words, wanted to laugh out loud, said,

"Go fuck yourself."

He gave a slight shake of his head—not anger, disappointment—then nodded to the men. They grabbed my arms, tied my hands behind me, pulled a cotton hood with no openings for eyes or mouth, over my head. I asked,

"What, you going to do me, too?"

I felt him close up, then a hand on my shoulder. He said,

"Jack, you will join us. As a demonstration of our belief in you, we've done you a special service this evening. I get the feeling you weren't paying attention in your history class, so here is a brief summary. The rebellion began when the hated Yeomen burned the church at Boolevogue. Fr Murphy, who had advised his parishioners to give up their arms, now told them to die courageously rather than be butchered. Once the rebels took Vinegar Hill, the whole country rose up. The most effective weapon they had was the pike. A solid mass of Wexford pikemen could only be broken by heavy artillery fire."

Then I was pulled to my feet and marched up some stairs, out to the street. I stumbled a few times. Being deprived of sight gives a complete sense of vulnerability. The van door opened and one of the guys said,

"Watch your step, Jack."

His voice was friendly, slightly amused. Within ten minutes we stopped and my hands were untied, the door opened and I was pushed out. Gaining my balance, I pulled off the hood as the van disappeared round a corner. I was close to the hotel and, save for a lone student, the streets were deserted. He looked as confused as I felt, with traces of vomit on his jeans. He said,

"Party town, eh?"

And wandered in the direction of Eyre Square.

I went into Bailey's, got to my room without seeing anyone and slumped on the bed. My head hurt but I didn't think it was serious. I could now tell Jeff I knew what he was talking about, and who else? Ridge? She'd say there was nothing to pursue. Or I could go to the top, to the superintendent of the guards.

Clancy and I had been friends, pulled early duties together. My career had ended and he'd gone to the very top. Our paths had crossed in the years since, and we were, if not enemies, at least adversaries. He viewed me with contempt. Whenever I'd tried to enlist his help, he'd laughed in my face. I got into bed, no plan formulated. I needn't have fretted; the superintendent was coming for me.

I was in a deep sleep when I felt myself pulled awake, muttered,

"What the fuck?"

Two guards towering over me. For a crazy moment, I thought it was the Pikemen again. The first said,

"Get dressed, Taylor."

I tried to shake the sleep away, and the second one pointed at my pillow, traces of blood, said,

"We better take that."

The room was in a mess; they'd already searched it. As I fumbled into my clothes, I asked,

"You want to tell me what the hell is going down?"

From a previous era, I'd stashed a Browning Automatic under the floorboards. Thank Christ, it wasn't that category of search.

Otherwise.

At least I'd quit my cocaine habit and no longer kept a stash. There wasn't even a bottle of booze. The first guard didn't answer my question, and when I was dressed, he snapped,

"Let's go."

The second one asked,

"Do we cuff him?"

Got the look from us both. As we went past the reception desk, I shook my head at Mrs Bailey and she refrained from comment. A squad car was waiting and a small crowd had gathered. Someone shouted,

"Is it Bin Laden?"

They put me in the back and we moved away. The guards were silent, with grim expressions. I knew from my own career as a guard that silence meant serious trouble. Anything less and the guards would chat, if not freely at least quietly. They didn't talk if they feared compromising the impending charge. I was rushed into the interview room, left alone. I asked,

"Could I get some tea?"

No tea.

Twenty minutes dragged by, then the door opened and Clancy entered, dressed in full regalia. The title of superintendent was still feeding his ego. His eyes were bleary, his skin mottled. The once formidable body had folded in on itself. He said,

"Taylor."

The tone was heavy. I asked,

"What's going on?"

He stared at me, then,

"Tim Coffey has been murdered."

"What?"

Ann Henderson's husband, who'd given me my limp.

Clancy asked,

"Where were you last night?"

And I felt relief flood in, said,

"I was with somebody."

He raised an eyebrow, asked,

"What time and the name?"

He took out a solid black notebook. I remembered those well. You better get everything down, especially times, dates, locations. If you had to do court, it might be your sole line of defence against a rampaging cross-examination. Clancy read through what I'd said, then walked out. Two hours passed and I knew it wasn't taking that long. The extra was to let me stew. When he eventually returned, he was not pleased, said,

"It checks out."

"So, I'm free to go?"

He pulled up a chair, turned it round, cowboy style, so he could rest his arms on the support: macho pose.

He said,

"You could have hired someone."

I let that notion float, then,

"You don't believe that, and you certainly know you can't prove it. Otherwise, I'd be hauled off to a cell and we wouldn't be having this conversation."

He rubbed his cheek with his hand and I asked,

"How was he killed?"

"With some sort of heavy metal pole, his skull caved in. I understand you and he had an . . . altercation."

He pronounced it with great care, almost delicately. It's a true guard word, conveying seriousness and an implied grandeur. Not for everyday usage. One you saved, savoured and unleashed at the appropriate time. I repeated,

"Altercation! I must look that up."

I did, later. The dictionary described it as "vehement dispute". I sat back in the chair, said,

"He beat the living shit out of me and, yes, with a hurley, but you know this already. Your officers investigated and, gee whiz, superintendent, guess what? Nothing came of it, not a damn thing."

He smiled and I noticed his teeth had been capped. No doubt it would enhance his media appearances. He was picturing the scene of Tim Coffey towering over me. I asked,

"Would you be interested at all in finding out who did kill Coffey?"

His smile didn't fade but the wattage had dimmed. He said,

"I like you for it, Jacky-boy."

I looked at him for a long time, wondering how it was we'd been such close friends and had moved so far from there. I said,

"The Pikemen."

He laughed out loud, a braying harsh noise, like the essence of nastiness, said,

"Pikemen, me arse. They're part of what the younger people like to call 'urban legend'."

But his body language had shifted, the deliberate casual pose was now on full alert. I said,

"Urban legend with guard shoes."

He shot off of the chair, snapped,

"Get out."

I stood up and for a mad moment thought we might shake hands. He flung the door open and I was out of there. I stood on the steps of the station, a brief shaft of sunlight on my face. From my left, a woman approached. Ann Henderson. Before I could formulate a single word, she spat in my face, then turned and walked away.

*I was sitting in Nestor's, a coffee going cold before me. I'd re-*lated to Jeff the whole series of events and he never once interrupted. He'd been polishing a glass, his head tilted to the side. The glass was shining. Time to time, I touched my left cheek, under the eye where the spittle had landed.

Jeff put the glass aside, said,

"We'll go after them."

"You and me?"

He looked round. The sentry was staring into space. He asked,

"You see anybody else?"

"No."

When I finally got back to the hotel, it was dark. Mrs Bailey asked,

"Are you all right?"

"I am."

"Good man."

I got upstairs and washed my face in cold water. Didn't help. The spittle had burned beyond the skin. Jeff had said he'd find out the identity of the Pikemen's leader. I'd asked,

"How?"

He shrugged.

"How hard can it be?"

"Heavy drinkers don't need to talk or cause trouble. There is a mutual agreement to just sit there and watch things slow down as you go numb, and nobody has anything to add, no commentary or footnote."

Chad Taylor, *Electric*

Next morning I felt, as the lines go:

"Drained of all

But memories of you."

I got the Synge books off the shelf and a pad and pen, tried to put him down on paper.

He was born in Dublin in 1871. His father, a barrister, died when Synge was in infancy. A student at Trinity, he later went to Paris. A meeting with W.B. Yeats was to be hugely influential. Yeats suggested he visit the Aran Islands, to learn how the Irish peasant lived and worked. From 1899 to 1902, he would visit there annually. The result was *The Aran Islands* in 1907, an account of his time there. Then there were the plays, the first, *In the Shadow of the Glen,* in 1903.

Riders to the Sea in 1904.

Well of the Saints in 1905.

Then of course, the famous riots in 1907 at the Abbey

when *The Playboy of the Western World* was unveiled. If nothing else, it ensured his fame.

That year, 1907, also saw his diatribe against the clergy, *The Tinker's Wedding.*

Synge became a director of the Abbey and 1909 brought *Poems and Translations.*

From 1897, he had suffered from Hodgkin's Disease. *Deirdre of the Sorrows* was begun but never completed as he entered his final days.

His realism and brazenly uncompromising portrayal of his people made him many enemies. You can say anything you like about the Irish, just don't say it directly.

I read through the notes and tried to grasp what a killer would find in Synge that would lead him to leave the man's work as his signature. I couldn't see it. I liked what Yeats said of Synge:

"He was the more hated because he gave his country what it needed, an unmoved heart."

That description, an unmoved heart, set up a deep chord in my soul. I'd known it all my troubled life.

I sat back, tried to get a picture of what the link could be between Synge and the Dramatist. I felt an idea forming when the phone rang.

Shit.

I picked up, said,

"Yeah?"

"Mr Taylor?"

"Yes."

"This is the matron of St Jude's, the nursing home?"

"Oh right, I was going to call you. I'll be moving my mother today."

Heard a confused voice in the background, her muffled reply, then,

"Today?"

"Yes, an ambulance will collect her I imagine."

Her breath came in short gasps. She asked,

"How on earth did you know so quickly?"

My turn to pause, then I asked,

"Know? Know what?"

"That your mother died twenty minutes ago."

I let the phone fall.

I don't know what it is about funerals and the weather. Well, Irish ones. We're used to rain. It's the west of Ireland; rain is what we do. But at funerals, every single one, it lashes down like it was personal.

My mother's was no exception.

Never let up, just teemed like a bastard. A large crowd, mostly people from her church. At the grave, her old retainer, my old nemesis, Fr Malachy droned on about dust to dust. I looked at the faces of the assembled mourners. They were appropriately sad. Course, the incessant downpour wasn't helping lift their spirits. As the only son, I was the chief mourner, but they managed to ignore me. If death brings a spirit of reconciliation, they weren't privy to it. Finally, Malachy was done and sprinkled holy water on the casket. He looked at me, or rather glared. I moved to grab a handful of soil and he shook his head. I thought "fuck you pal" and let it fall on the coffin. The gravediggers began to lower my mother and signalled me to participate. She was no weight, no weight at all.

The task completed, I stepped back and Margaret took my hand. Malachy noticed and frowned. I gripped her fingers tight. Ridge, across from us, blessed herself and moved away.

I cleared my throat, said,

"Um, thank you for coming. I've booked Hollywood's Bar, for . . . um . . . food, refreshments . . . you're all invited . . . thank you."

And felt like a horse's ass.

They didn't come.

Just Margaret, Ridge and tables of sandwiches, canisters of tea, coffee and five bar staff. Eventually, the bar manager, getting antsy, asked,

"Are you expecting more . . . guests?"

I shook my head.

Margaret took a sandwich. It left the mountain of food unmoved. She attempted a bite, asked,

"Your friend, the one who owns the bar?"

"Jeff, and his wife Cathy."

She was nervous, sorry she'd mentioned them, and I said,

"They didn't show."

I offered no explanation as I had none. Ridge, toying with an orange juice, almost looked pretty. A dark suit, with a fashionably cut skirt, white blouse with a hint of cleavage. Close up, the cut of the outfit was poor; whatever else, Ridge always shopped cheap. I said,

"You look nice."

Our relationship wasn't about to develop intimacy because of the situation. She gave me the usual icy look, said,

"It's a funeral, who looks nice?"

She said she was due on duty, and I walked her to the door. I said,

"Thanks for coming."

No give. She faced me, asked,

"Did you have him killed?"

"Tim Coffey?"

She stared at me and I protested,

"No, of course not. Jeez, give me a break."

She looked towards Margaret, said,

"I pity her."

I was all out of diplomacy.

She added,

"You still carry a torch for the new widow, Ann Coffey, or is it Henderson?"

I thought it was a cheap shot, to match the cheap clothes, went,

"That's a bit strong. I like Margaret."

She let her mouth twist down, an ugly gesture, turned to go, said,

"What's not to like?"

*In Galway, more and more, you see families of eastern Europe-*ans, trailing the streets with stunned expressions. The father in imitation black leather jacket, the mother a few steps behind with the old Dunne's shopping bags and the young kids in rip-off designer sports shirts. Adidas or Nike spelt incorrectly. Such a family was passing and I invited them in, said,

"Eat, eat."

Two winos, a level above wet despair, I also gathered. Got them behind large Jamesons, and they lined their pockets with the sandwiches. The manager raised his eyes to heaven, then stared at his watch. It seemed to yield scant comfort. The door was flung open and, trailing cigarette smoke, Fr Malachy marched in, went to the counter, ordered a large Paddy. I was never sure if he liked my mother, but he spent an inordinate amount of time in her company. I was sure of his loathing for me. Margaret and I watched him approach us. He threw a withering look at the crowd eating from the buffet, said,

"Friends of yours no doubt."

I put out my hand but he ignored it, stared at Margaret, asked,

"Are you a Galway girl?"

Girl!

Her voice adopted the centuries old lower tone that women have for the clergy. She said,

"I am, Father."

He threw back the whiskey, his cheeks crimson, asked,

"And what in the Lord's name are you doing with this yoke?"

Before she could reply, I said,

"I appreciate your help to my mother but watch your mouth."

He rounded on me, spittle staining his black lapels, said,

"Your mother, God rest her, is free of you at last."

Walloping a priest is never going to be socially acceptable. Popular maybe, but not openly condoned. I was considering it but reached for my wallet, said,

"You'll need paying."

His eyes jumping, he was almost glad I'd given him an opening. He said,

"Money! From the likes of you? I'd go to England before I'd let that happen."

"Is that a no?"

I heard someone approach, turned to see Sergeant

Keogh, in a dark suit. One of the few guards from my old days who still acknowledged me. He gave the classic line of Irish sympathy,

"I'm sorry for your trouble."

I got him a drink and we moved to the end of the bar. I glanced back to see Malachy offering Margaret a cigarette, a fresh drink in his fist.

Keogh asked,

"Did she go easy?"

Assuming he meant my mother, I said,

"She never did anything easy in her life."

He nodded, then,

"You'll miss her though."

He was trying to be nice so I let it slide. I asked,

"You ever hear of the Pikemen?"

His eyes roared Yes, and he answered,

"People are tired of the legal way of dealing with things."

He gave a short laugh, added,

"Or should I say not dealing with them."

I waited and he considered, then,

"There's only a few of them. If it weren't for their leader, they'd fade away."

Mrs Bailey and Janet had attended the funeral mass and sent large bouquets of flowers. I was glad they weren't here to see the shambles of a reception.

The sergeant finished his drink, said,

"I better get a move on, Jack."

"Thanks for coming."

The family of non-nationals had gone and all of the food. The winos were shaping up to fight each other. I said,

"Time to go, lads."

And I slipped them a bottle of Irish, one of them asked,

"Was it a wedding?"

"No, a funeral."

He suddenly threw his arms round me, his body odour almost overwhelming as he near crushed me, said,

"You be strong now, big guy."

As they were leaving, he turned, made the sign of the cross, said,

"God bless all here."

" 'Burglary, for the District Court,' Waters said. 'I imagine the Grand Jury'll be getting a better variety of charges. Let's see, two murders, three robberies, burglary in all them bankers' houses, probably gun-running, stolen car, conspiracy. Did I leave something out?' 'Blasphemy,' Foley said, 'I always wanted to charge a guy with blasphemy.' "

George V. Higgins, *The Friends of Eddie Coyle*

I woke the morning after the funeral, amazed I hadn't drunk.
Hadn't even had a cigarette. Was this grace? Sure didn't feel
very blessed. Dark snakes coiled and twisted in my mind.
The ferocious guilt about my mother was a lash of epic
proportions. Trying to block out the pictures of her in that
cot, left to decay in the knacker's yard.

Jesus, who wouldn't drink? Alas, there wasn't enough
Jameson in the world to erase the stench of my abandonment. I had left her to waste away.

I trolled through the data of my present.

Tim Coffey, murdered on my account. A nutcase, ob-
sessed with Synge, who'd killed two girls and was playing
mind games. Not to mention the bloody vigilantes—
Pikemen for Chrissakes.

I brewed some coffee, told myself I could really savour it
without the shield of nicotine. The stillness in the room

was startling. Moved, turned on the radio, caught the tail end of Coldplay's "Yellow".

That was definitely today's colour.

The news followed. Robin Cook had resigned from Blair's government. Saddam Hussein had been given seventy-two hours to leave Iran. The second UN resolution was no longer relevant. War was coming, lethal and soon. Then the local news: three bodies had been taken out of the canal, one was a black man.

Then,

"In Kinvara, a Galwayman has been seriously injured in a hit and run. He was well known in the area as president of the Vinegar Hill Association."

I took a deep breath.

President of the Vinegar Hill Association? The most famous event in the rebellion of 1798, the hour of the pikemen. I knew a girl at Galway Bay FM and rang her, wrangled the name of the victim from her. Ted Buckley. Then I got the number of the hospital, called and asked for intensive care, got put through to the nursing sister, said,

"Good morning, this is Sean Buckley. My brother Ted was brought in last night."

"Yes?"

"How is he doing?"

"He sustained serious injuries, Mr Buckley. His back is broken and his legs; he has head injuries, too."

"Oh God."

"Shall I put you through to the doctor?"

"Um, no. Is his wife there?"

I could hear the dawning suspicion. She went,

"Mr Buckley is single. Who did you say you were again?"

I hung up.

Back to the phone directory and there he was:

> Edward Buckley
> 21, Corrib Park
> Galway

Underneath was "Vinegar Hill Association, situated at Kinvara".

Operated it from home with a branch in Kinvara. I thought back to my hooded drive in the van, ten minutes or so. I put on my all-weather coat and figured the walk would be good for my limp. Took me twenty minutes to get to Corrib Park, and it was a hive of activity. People everywhere, which could only be a good thing. I walked up to No. 21, rang the doorbell, hoping to hell he didn't have a dog. No sound. I moved round to the back and began to move bins, checking the neighbouring houses for watchers. No indication. I used my elbow, hard and fast, broke a pane, got the window open and climbed in. If a neighbour was calling the guards, I'd know real soon. I was in the kitchen, which had that fussy tidiness of a bachelor. I recognised the signs from my years of aloneness. Single guys go either way. Slob or neat-compulsive, and he was definitely the latter. Not even a cup draining on the sink.

The floor spotless, tea cloths folded, lined regimentally. I almost felt for him. Checked my watch, fifteen minutes, and let out my breath. No guards. Went through the other rooms. Same deal, tidy as obsession. A bookcase, all Irish history, concentrating on 1798. A heavy framed drawing of a priest above the fireplace—Fr Murphy, hero of the rebellion.

Found a door to the basement, hit the wall switch and went down. Here it was, the long wooden table, the pikes on the wall. I whispered,

"Gotcha."

Back upstairs, I collected all the paper I could and pulled down the linen curtains. Took me a time and my knee ached, but finally I'd laid a line of paper and clothes from the kitchen to the basement. I remembered his nicotine-stained teeth and, in the press beneath the sink, found lighter fluid. Doused the trail of paper, concentrating on the kitchen and trail end in the basement. Matches were stacked neatly alongside a gas stove. I opened the kitchen door, lit a match, let it drop, said,

"Whoosh."

Lawrence Block, in Out on the Cutting Edge, *has his character,* Matt Scudder, at an AA meeting where a woman recounts how she used to take the first drink of the day as soon as her husband left for work. She kept the vodka bottle under the sink, in a container that had previously held oven cleaner.

"The first time I told this story," she said, "a woman said, 'Oh dear Jesus, suppose you grabbed the wrong jar and drank the real oven cleaner.'

" 'Honey,' I told her, 'get real, will you? There was no wrong jar. There was no real oven cleaner. I lived in that house for thirteen years and I never cleaned the oven.'

"Anyway," she said "that was my social drinking."

I love that story.

Ran it through my mind two days later as I entered Nestor's. The sentry was at the bar, sunk in gloom, muttered,

"The bombing's begun."

Cathy was tending bar, a very rare occurrence. I leaned on the counter, asked,

"Where's himself?"

"He had to meet somebody."

She assessed me, said,

"I am very sorry for your mother. Jeff was out of town, and I couldn't get a babysitter."

I nodded. The sentry perked up, asked,

"Did somebody die?"

We didn't answer him. Cathy asked if I wanted a coffee and I declined. I was running options in my head and then she added,

"How is Stewart?"

It took me a moment to focus, then I said,

"He's in jail, how did you think he'd be?"

She mulled it over, asked,

"Are you working for him?"

"Good question."

She began to polish the counter. It was already buffed to a professional level. Course it meant I had to move my elbow and step back. She said,

"I dropped the dime."

"What?"

"On Stewart. I gave him up."

I was stunned, tried to get a handle on it, said,

"You called the guards?"

"Sure, the drug squad."

Her face as she said this was neutral, no emotion showing. I thought of Sinéad O'Connor blowing the whistle
on Shane McGowan. I almost stammered, got out,

"He was your friend."

She gave a brief noise of disdain, said,

"He was a drug dealer; they don't do friendships."

And neither, I thought, do you. Said,

"The poor bastard got six years."

"Sufficient time to clean up, don't you think?"

I was too rattled to say what I thought, tried,

"See you later."

I was at the door when she called,

"We'll get a mass card for your mother."

I could hardly wait.

Round the back of the pub is a shed/garage where Jeff
keeps his beloved Harley. Next to Cathy and their daughter, it is his most treasured possession. A soft-tail custom, he
keeps it in immaculate condition, every spare moment
given to polishing, cleaning and maintenance. The few
times I'd seen it, the chrome and metal were shining. You
want to hear true passion, ask him about the bike. He
moves to another level as he extols the machine. To try and
grasp the zeal, I'd read Gary Paulsen's *Pilgrimage on a Steel
Ride*. I got some notion of the sheer love a Harley inspires
but far from a complete understanding. Harley freaks are
simply another species. Jeff had told me a Harley breaks
down more times and has more problems than all other
bikes put together. I'd asked,

"Why bother?"

And his look of horror as he gasped,

"Man, they're a thoroughbred. You don't exchange the best because they're finely tuned. It's what makes them great."

The shed wasn't locked and I pulled open the door, hit the light switch. The Harley was in the centre, looking fucked. I bent down, got a look at the front. The metal was heavily dented, mud and dirt streaked along the side. The rim of the heavy tire was almost cut open. Heard a voice,

"Snooping on me, Jack?"

I stood, turned to face Jeff. In his right hand, he held a heavy wrench. A moment passed between us that I don't ever want to analyse.

I indicated the bike, asked,

"Bit of an accident?"

He dropped the wrench, the sound ugly against the stone floor. He moved towards me but the aggression had evaporated, said,

"It wasn't an accident, but you know that already."

I wished I still smoked; it was definitely a nicotine moment. I said,

"You could have killed him, Jeff."

He nodded, his left hand reaching out to the bike, almost caressing it, said,

"I thought I had."

I'd hoped for a denial and maybe I'd have gone along. I asked,

"How did you find him?"

He gave me a surprised look, then,

"I run a pub, everybody talks. A few extra shots of Scotch, on the house, you learn all you need."

Then he leaned against the bike, weariness on his face, asked,

"You going to turn me in?"

I was going to say, that's what your wife does, but turned to leave, said,

"I'm going to pretend you didn't say that."

He waited a moment then,

"He deserved it."

I had no reply.

"Not even the great weather could hide the disorder and deep sorrow here, as the pastoral degenerated into unplanned urban sprawl. I could almost smell the bitter energies of change and failure.
I seemed to be in some sort of downhill tumble myself, going from bad to worse as I stumbled through the transition from a semi-employed private eye to a solid citizen and back down again."

James Crumley, *The Final Country*

Four weeks went by in a blur of pain, guilt, remorse, confusion. I couldn't get past the way my mother had died. Alone, abandoned and afraid. I didn't drink or dope or nicotine. The three lethal addictions preyed constantly, but I don't know why I didn't succumb. I once heard if you want to change your life, your attitude, you begin by altering your behaviour. Do the opposite to what you used to do and change will come down the pike. So instead of embracing my usual destruction, I stayed busy. Re-interviewing the students, friends, acquaintances of the dead girls. Even did coffee with Ronan Wall, to see what might shake loose.

Nothing did.

I read Synge, read him twice. The near breakthrough I had before my mother's death remained elusive, tantalisingly out of reach. Ronan Wall continued to tease and carefully provoke. He knew I wanted him for the frame but it wasn't happening. I took Margaret out regularly but it was eroding. I thought I was covering well, acting almost normal, till she eventually asked,

"Where are you, Jack?"

We'd been to see the Brazilian *City of God,* of which I recall nothing. After, we'd gone to Brennan's Yard, got a late supper. Thick brown crusted sandwiches, pot of tea. I ate without taste. To her question, I said,

"I was thinking about Baghdad, the intense horrific pictures I've seen on CNN."

I wasn't.

She shook her head, said,

"No, you weren't."

It was far too late and too blatant a lie to give the answer women most hope for . . . "I was thinking of you, dear." Truth to tell, I was nowhere, in the place of white noise, grey visions. She said, taking my hand,

"You're in a dead place."

I knew the truth of that. The day before, I'd watched Ireland beat Georgia and only briefly engaged when a knife was thrown, hitting Kilbane on the ear. Sunday, I sat through the Six Nations, Ireland vs England, in a veritable trance. Played in Lansdowne Road, it was a huge national event, and I felt removed.

I took my hand away from Margaret's, muttered,

"I'll snap out if it."

No escape. She whispered sadly,

"I sure hope so, Jack."

Then, pushing the sandwiches away, she asked,

"Are you talking to anyone?"

"To Cathy . . . and Jeff."

Vaguely true.

I was still babysitting for them. Jeff was cool, kept our conversation to the minimum. Cathy, more animated, was happy at how I'd bonded with her child.

And bonded I had.

I continued to read to her, and her face lit up as I produced a fresh book. I don't know how much she understood, but her eyes danced with knowledge. Three years of age with a button nose, brown eyes, mischievous mouth, I could have stared at her for hours. She intrigued me. Here was a child, with Down's syndrome, deemed by the world as damaged, less than handicapped. Yet, she had a vitality that energised even my cynical spirit. During those frozen weeks after my mother's death, the times with Serena May were the only brightness I experienced. She had a smile to die for, as innocent in life as I was guilty. That would be our undoing. Per custom, we used the room above the pub and a large window looked out over Forster Street. By craning our necks, Serena in my arms, we could see Eyre Square. I'd tell her of Pádraic Ó Conaire's statue at the top and the metal cannons flanking him. I skipped over the winos huddled at the fountain. Then I'd put her down and she'd zoom around the room with joy. It could only be a short time till she walked. Cathy took it very hard that other children walked at a year or even ten months. Here was her daughter, over three and still scrambling on all fours. The sentry had once remarked,

"That child, she's an old soul."

I was so surprised that I went,

"What?"

"She's been here before."

And returned to contemplating his half full glass of porter. I wanted to ask if he believed in reincarnation but he was all done. Cathy seemed to appreciate the amount of time I gave to Serena, said,

"Jack, this is such a help."

"No big thing."

It wasn't.

I went to visit Ted Buckley. He was encased in plaster, pulleys holding an arm and leg suspended. His eyes were open and they hardened as I approached. I said

"How you doing there, Ted?"

He tried to act like I was a stranger, but immobile in a bed, how many ways can you fake it?

"I know you?"

"Jack Taylor."

The nicotine teeth locked down, and I didn't think agitation was going to do his condition much good.

"That supposed to mean something?"

I pulled up a chair, straddled it. If Superintendent Clancy could do it, then hell, why not?

"Ah, does this mean I can't join you, not be a vigilante?"

He tried to shift his head as if seeking help, then said,

"I don't know what you're talking about."

I let that hang for a bit, then,

"You killed a guard."

Spittle lit the corners of his lips. The frustration of being immobile was eating him hard. He said,

"Prove it."

I stood up, said,

"Heard you had a fire."

He managed to move the leg in traction but it was a feeble gesture. He said,

"You were in my home?"

I shrugged, turned to go, added,

"Not me, pal. I'd say vigilantes."

My limp seemed to have worsened, but I blamed the hospital vibe. A doctor in his fifties approached, asked,

"You were visiting Mr Buckley?"

"I was."

He had a chart—don't they always?—peered at it and made medical noises, then,

"It's very sad, but I don't think Mr Buckley will walk again."

I nodded, my face grave. He asked,

"Will you be visiting regularly?"

"Absolutely, to be sure your prognosis is right."

His head came up, a challenge in his eyes, said,

"I can tell you, Mr . . . ? I didn't get your name."

"I didn't give it."

"Ah, well, I can assure you it's very unlikely the patient will ever be mobile again."

I stared at him, made some medical noises of my own, then,

"I'm going to take that as a promise."

Downstairs, the main hall was hectic with activity. The last time I'd been here, I had the disastrous meeting with Ann Henderson. I went to the café and saw they were advertising every type of designer coffee. I ordered a cappuccino without the chocolate sprinkle. The girl said,

"You mean latte?"

"If I wanted latte, you think I wouldn't have ordered that?"

She gave me the look. After Buckley, I could take it and she backed off, got the coffee and, to coin a vigilante phrase, "charged me an arm and a leg". I found a free table, sat down. The radio was playing Keith Finnegan fielding a discussion on the use of Shannon Airport by the American troops. Then he said listeners had requested a song by the Dixie Chicks from their new album *Home,* a track about Vietnam but just as relevant to Iraq. I was listening to that when a porter approached, launched,

"I hope you're not even considering smoking?"

He'd taken me completely by surprise and I went,

"What?"

"This whole area is a no smoking zone."

He was fired up, ready to rock 'n' roll. I recognised him but couldn't find a name. I said,

"I don't smoke."

How odd that sounded. He wasn't buying, snapped,

"I remember you, in the corridors, smoking in the alcove."

I let out my breath, asked,

"Do me a favour, pal?"

"Favour, what favour?"

"Fuck off."

He did.

The Dixie Chicks lingered in my head as I walked down by NUI. Students were milling round the canal, and I thought of the dead girls. It didn't seem like I was ever going to solve that. At the church, I paused, stared at the stained glass windows. They didn't provide any inspiration. I muttered,

"Windows. Just coloured glass."

I returned to the hotel. Mrs Bailey, looking frail, almost delicate, was near swamped in paperwork. Though I wanted to be alone, to go into myself and basically sulk, I stopped, asked,

"Are you OK, Mrs B?"

She raised her head and it pained me to glimpse her skull through the thinning hair. That grieved me so. I noticed the profusion of liver spots on her hands and could only hazard a guess at her age. Someone had attempted to perm her hair and made a shocking mess, as if half way through they decided,

"Fuck this, it's a shambles."

And it was.

She said,

"I don't want to burden you, Mr Taylor, what with your recent loss."

I wanted to agree, slip away to my room, but I stayed, asked,

"How about I buy you a drink, a big fat warm whiskey, with cloves, sugar . . . hell, we'll shoot the works."

She smiled like a young girl for a moment, almost flirtatious, and I realised how much she meant to me. Course, my mother's death had left me vulnerable, but this woman had stood by me through all manner of shit storms. Each time I got sober or clean then crashed, she never judged me. Kept a room always available. When I fucked off to London, to Hidden Valley, and came literally limping back, she welcomed me.

Top that.

She asked,

"Who'll mind the desk?"

I indicated the paperwork, said,

"With some luck, it will be stolen."

She was sold.

Came out from behind the desk and, lo and behold, linked my arm. No one links you like a Galway woman. I felt . . . gallant? How often are you going to see that description? I moved towards the door and she protested, went,

"Oh no, I don't go out any more."

"What?"

"It's too dangerous."

I couldn't argue with that; it was bloody lethal out there, I had the limp to prove it. She added,

"Anyway, if I'm going to have a drink, I'd prefer to give the custom to myself."

Despite the length of time I'd been at the hotel, I think I'd only ever once been in the bar. The don't-shit-on-your-own-doorstep syndrome. My kind of pub though: dark, smoky, old, lived in. Serious drinkers had drunk very seriously here. You could feel the vibe, the one that whispered,

"If you want fancy drinks, fuck off."

This was your pint of plain and a ball of malt, and if you needed that translated, you were definitely in the wrong place.

"While the grave was being opened the women sat down among the flat tombstones, bordered with a pale fringe of early bracken, and began the wild keen, or crying for the dead. Each old woman, as she took her turn in the leading recitative, seemed possessed for the moment with a profound ecstasy of grief, swaying to and fro, and bending her forehead to the stone before her, while she called out to the dead with a perpetually recurring chant of sobs."

J.M. Synge, *The Aran Islands*

There was no one tending the bar. In Ireland, you find the strangest items in pubs, but an unmanned counter isn't one of them. I looked at Mrs Bailey and she said,

"I'll do it."

I had to ask,

"Doesn't anyone actually work it?"

She gave a deep sigh, said,

"We have a fellah, but he tends to be his own best customer. We don't have much business, so I usually do it myself."

I marched her to a table, sat her down, bowed, asked,

"What would Madam care to imbibe?"

She was delighted, went,

"Something sweet."

I glanced back at the dusty but well-stocked shelves. I said,

"Might I suggest a schooner of sherry?"

She shook her head, said,

"That's an old woman's drink. I don't want to be old for a minute."

And who could blame her? I said,

"Crème de menthe?"

She clapped her hands, said,

"Perfect."

I went behind the bar and stood transfixed, an alcoholic in front of the guns. All the lethal boyos were up there, optics in place: Jameson, Paddy, Black Bush. In jig time, I could have a double up, gone and walloped. I looked at Mrs Bailey. She wasn't clocking me. From a ream of newspapers on the table before her, she'd selected the *Galway Advertiser* and was flicking through it. I poured her a large, got a Galway sparkling water for myself and left twenty euro on the till. No free drinks this day. Went over and sat opposite her, raised my glass and we clinked. I said,

"Sláinte amach."

"Leat féin."

She took a delicate sip, said,

"That's great stuff."

We savoured a moment of silence, not uncomfortable, then I asked,

"What's troubling you, Mrs B?"

She folded her hands in her lap, then,

"They're squeezing me out. Developers, creditors, a whole crowd of them. I'm sinking and I'm afraid I'll have to sell."

One more Galway institution to be drowned beneath progress, everything decent and fine and, yes, old was being demolished. She asked,

"Did you know they are going to cut down the trees on Eyre Square?"

"What?"

"They say they'll replace them."

She gave a strangled sound, added,

"I don't understand it. You cut down healthy trees and then replace them?"

She was lost for words till she near exploded.

"'Tis blasphemy!"

I'd caught the aroma of the *crème de menthe*. Sure it was sweet, but the underlay of alcohol was as strong as loss. I got a massive compulsion to leap the counter, put my mouth under an optic and squeeze till doomsday. I shuddered and she laid her hand on mine, a gentle touch, asked,

"Are you cold, *a mhic*?"

A mhic! The Irish for son. In my youth, you heard it all the time. Back in the Claddagh, the old people used it still. A term of affection and endearment, sometimes scolding but never harsh. I said,

"Must be a draught."

She looked round, seeing what ghosts I'd never know. I had my own crew to carry. She said,

"Of course, they'll knock it down, put up some monstrosity, but, please God, I'll be gone to my rest. You know

what, Mr Taylor, you can live past your time and that's a
sorrow."

I thought of Synge, his *Deirdre of the Sorrows*. Somehow,
it always came back to that play, the passage highlighted in
red I'd memorised. Deirdre, in the play, is crouching and
swaying as she keens. She makes a straight speech to the
dead, remembering the comforts of her time with them
and the sheer despair of having them no more. It reached
me in ways I could never have anticipated. The startling realisation, bizarre as it sounds, that the Dramatist was speaking to me . . . *perhaps trying to teach me something.*

It goes:

It's you three will not see age or death coming; you that were
my company when the fires on the hilltops were put out and
the stars were our friends only. I'll turn my thoughts back
from this night—that's pitiful for want of pity—to the time
it was your rods and cloaks made a little tent for me where
there'd be a birch tree making shelter, and on a dry stone;
though from this day my own fingers will be making a tent
for me, spreading out my hairs and they knotted with the
rain.

Despite myself, I was beginning to appreciate Synge. His
language sang to the primeval part of my ancestry, to the
very core of what made me Irish. Or maybe it had been
too long since I got drunk. I said aloud,

"That's pitiful for want of pity."

Mrs Bailey gasped, stared at me, said,

"Isn't that a beautiful thought—sad but true."

The sparkle was dying in my glass of water. I said,

"It's by Synge."

She nodded, then,

"There was a holy row when his play was at the Abbey."

"You're familiar with him?"

"I'm familiar with rows."

Janet, the chambermaid, stuck her head in the door, said,

"Mrs B, you're wanted on the phone."

She touched my arm, said,

"I'll be back in a tick. I enjoy your company."

She rose from the chair with difficulty, her bones creaking. I flipped through the *Galway Advertiser,* began to read about the line-up for the forthcoming Cuirt Festival of Literature. Turned the page and was looking at photos without registering much, hadn't realised Janet was peering over my shoulder, till she exclaimed,

"There's your friend!"

I nearly jumped, went,

"What?"

She leaned over, put her finger on a photo, said,

"There, that's the man I met outside your room. He was carrying a large plastic bag. Lovely manners he had."

I tried to concentrate, looked at a photo of a heavyset man with a distinguished appearance and a mane of thick white hair presenting a prize to a student. Underneath was the caption:

"Professor O'Shea of the English Dept at NUI presenting the prize for best essay to his student, Conor Smith."

O'Shea . . . the name rang some chord. First I had to pin
down Janet, asked,

"Tell me about . . . my friend. Don't leave anything
out."

She was worried, creases down her already impossibly
lined face, went,

"Did I do wrong?"

"No, no, he wanted to surprise me."

Did he ever.

She frowned, then,

"It was a while ago. I'd been hoovering on the top floor,
came down to get some bin liners and saw him outside
your door. He asked if that was your room, said that you
were old friends, that he'd wait a bit, see if you returned.
He had a grand way of talking, you'd know he was a professional man, and gorgeous cologne."

I could see him, prodded,

"And the bag, did you see what was in it?"

Her eyes brightened.

"Now that was odd. I got the impression it was a flower
or plant. He held it close to his chest, like he was trying to
hide it. Was it flowers?"

"It was, sort of."

It didn't look like Mrs Bailey was returning any time
soon so I took her drink, handed it to Janet, said,

"Your good health."

"Oh, I don't know if I should. It makes me giddy."

I gave her my best smile, all false sincerity, said,

"Giddy is good."

That night, tossing and turning, something was trying to surface. Then I sat up: that time in Charlie Byrne's, when Vinny introduced me to the professor—the Synge expert—it was him, the man in the photo.

Rang Vinny at Charlie Byrne's bookshop. He asked,

"Jack, how's the Synge studies going?"

"Good. Listen, do you remember Professor O'Shea?"

"Of course I do. I introduced you to him in here: he's the expert on Synge. You should really go and have a talk with him if you want detailed insight."

"That's what I want all right."

Vinny hesitated then,

"Use a bit of tact, Jack."

"What?"

"His wife died a few years back and they were childless. I think he's probably lonely."

"I know how that goes."

"We got some new stock in: Daniel Buckman, K.T. Mc-Caffrey, John Straley, Declan Burke, like that."

"Put them aside for me."

"Don't I always?"

"I owe you a pint."

"You owe me a fleet of pints."

Click.

The telephone directory had the professor listed.

29, The Crescent

Galway

Old Galway, maybe old money.

I intended finding out, and soon.

"From the depths of the mirror, a corpse gazed back at me. The look in his eyes, as they stared into mine, has never left me."

Elie Wiesel, *Night, Dawn, the Accident*

Early morning, I listened to the news. Ferocious fighting on the outskirts of Baghdad. The Americans had taken the airport and renamed it Baghdad International.

What's in a name?

I rang NUI and asked if I might speak to the professor, make an appointment maybe. Difficult, as he'd a heavy agenda of lectures, seminars, meetings. He should be free near 4:30 p.m. I hung up.

That gave me the day.

I wore black jeans, black T and my garda all-weather overcoat. In my pockets, I put screwdrivers, the dead girls' photos and *Deirdre of the Sorrows.* It was a beautiful spring day, and as I walked towards Dominic Street, I had to take my coat off. My limp was definitely improving. I remembered Tim Coffey saying that kids would call me "Johnny the limp". Well, it hadn't happened.

The Crescent was impressive: old houses, large gardens

with the houses well back from the road. Most were occupied by doctors and consultants. I found No. 29 and took a moment. It was a dark house with an air of neglect, large hedges running along both sides so no neighbourly chats. Ivy crept along the front of the building and needed trimming. It wasn't derelict but had definitely seen better days. I opened the gate and walked boldly up the path. On one of the other houses I'd seen the notice "Neighbourhood Watch".

Always an invitation to thieves. When they don't warn you, that's the time to worry.

I avoided the front door, went along the side and found a garage joined to the house.

OK.

Using the screwdriver, I had the ancient lock off in a moment. No doubt about it, I was becoming a habitual burglar. In the garage was a pile of junk, rusted lawnmower, rakes and shovels. All looking as if they hadn't been touched in years. A thick rope was coiled on a shelf, and I picked it up, uncoiled it, then let it lie. Went through to the main house. Unlike the Pikemen's leader, Ted Buckley, here was a home gone to rack and ruin. Despite an air of mustiness and decay, dust everywhere, I couldn't help admiring the place. An air of grandeur, high ceilings, intricate designs and expensive carpets. I know a good rug because when you've lived with lino and cheap coverings, you get a sense of the better deal. The kitchen had black oak furniture and one of those fine kitchen tables like a butcher's block. Cups, mugs, plates were piled in the sink. None of the modern conveniences—no dishwasher, microwave, not even a toaster. Maybe he used a fork, held the bread in front of a two-bar fire. That vision didn't play, not with the photo of the man I'd seen in the *Advertiser.* The floor needed a serious sweep. I did spot a coffee machine, the real beans deal.

I found what I took to be his study, and it was heavy with the smell of pipe tobacco. I had to open a window—the stench was overwhelming—though I only opened it a little lest he return prematurely. Heavy drapes on the windows were half closed, and I pulled them back to have some light.

And gasped.

Wall-to-wall books. That was the other smell, the nectar of old volumes. There was even one of those movable ladders beloved of your true bibliophile. Four shelves devoted to Synge, and they looked like first editions. Though well used, they were in good condition, lovingly cared for. A computer on the desk, an old Macintosh. I turned to the sideboard and saw heavy silver-framed photos. The dead wife in two and then a young man I recognised. I felt dizzy, tried to get my mind in gear. I knew him. Niall O'Shea, who'd been horseplaying outside my childhood home; my father had broken his jaw. Niall O'Shea who had climbed the crane at the docks, sailed off.

Jesus.

I sat at the professor's desk and opened the drawers. A

sheet of paper with the lines from *Deirdre of the Sorrows* I'd memorised, that began:

"It's you three will not see age or death coming."

Fuck.

Opened the bottom drawer and found a green folder with bold black letters on the front:

THE DRAMATIST

My mind was reeling. Here I was solving a case, piece by piece, actually doing decent investigative work, and I felt wretched. In the folder were three photos. The first two I recognised:

Sarah Bradley

Karen Lowe

On the backs, in the same bold print, was,

AT PEACE

The third, I didn't know, and with a sense of dread I looked at the back:

SOON

I nearly had it all. She was next, to be the third that wouldn't "see age or death coming".

I stood up and paced, opened a press. It held bottles of Glenfiddich, Glenlivet, Jameson, Black Bushmills. Ah.

I shut the press quickly. On the table was a pipe rack, with well-used briars and a *dúidín* holding centre stage. Used for years by the peasants on Aran and a great favourite with tourists. They'd been remaking them for the Americans. Word was that heads were very partial for their use with weed. This one was an old, clay tube, and bore in tiny letters along the stem:

j.m.s.

Was it possible?

I went into the kitchen, spent the next half hour grinding coffee beans, getting the brew just so. Set it to go. Few aromas match the real scent of genuine coffee. It almost comforted me. I never take sugar but searched for some now. I was feeling weak and definitely needed the rush. Ceramic mugs, by Don Knox, hand crafted. What they were was dirty, so I rinsed and scrubbed one diligently. Poured the brew and put heaped spoonfuls of sugar in. Didn't bother seeking milk. Black was how I was. Drank it off, sweet and scalding, and sure enough, the jolt hit me fast. Not so much energised as focused. I half filled the mug again and went to the garage. Sipping the liquid, I studied the roof. A thick beam of wood ran end to end. I put the mug down, got the rope, and it took three attempts to get it over the beam.

Then I pulled up a stool and began to fasten the noose.

I returned to the study, closed the window and refixed the heavy drape. Then I sat in the professor's chair, settled to wait. The light was fading when I heard the key in the door. Then wheezing and laboured breathing and the sound of a heavy briefcase hitting the floor. He came into the study and hit the light switch. His first response was shock, but he collected himself rapidly, gave a knowing smile, said,

"Jack Taylor, I presume."

He was a big man, wearing a wool suit that had been expensive once. Now, it was merely shabby. He'd an off-white shirt with a tie askew, and his long white hair was rumpled, with dandruff on his shoulders. He wasn't unlike the English actor Brian Cox, who'd played the first Hannibal Lector in the underrated *Manhunter*. A contained strength, rugged face, pitted skin and bloodshot eyes. They were vibrant though, revealing a fierce intelligence. He was carrying a brown bag with "McCambridge's" on the side. From their deli I'd guess. As I said, old Galway.

He put the bag down, said,

"I'm going to have a drink, care to join me? . . . Or are you continuing your fragile sobriety?"

I stared at him and he said,

"I'll take that as a no."

He moved to the press, took out a heavy Galway Crystal tumbler and splashed in a generous amount of Glenlivet, held it up to the light, said,

"*Go n-éiri an bóthar leat.*"

And knocked it back, refilled. I said,

"Slow down, Prof, I want you reasonably coherent."

He gave a short laugh.

"There is no coherence. Haven't you been listening to the news?"

I placed the girls' photos on the desk, said,

"You decided to spare these poor creatures all that?"

He nodded, pleased.

"My students, creatures of innocence the world wanted to ruin and corrupt, but not now. I knew about the drug dealer, that scum, Stewart; it was fitting that his sister be selected. The second girl, she smoked pot. Bet you didn't know that, did you?"

He sat in the chair opposite, no tension in his body, relaxed, as if dealing with a not too bright student. I said,

"You decided to involve me because of your brother . . . what, you think my father's punch led him to suicide, all those years later?"

He reached for one of his pipes, a worn briar, took a leather pouch from his jacket, began to fill the bowl, said,

"Clan! Leaves a most fragrant aroma. How simplistic you are. Yes, my brother was shamed by your father's action. Did it lead to his suicide? Perhaps. As you know, some hurts can never be wiped away. It did lead me to take an active interest in your family. I have followed your precarious career with . . . how shall I say . . . bemusement. I learnt of your visiting that dregs of humanity, the drug dealer, from Superintendent Clancy; the guards at Mountjoy were enraged that you'd visited him."

I stood up, walked over to the window. His eyes were too intense, too penetrating. I said,

"Rationalise all you like, you murdered two girls."

His voice rose, just a timbre, but I got a sense of how fine a lecturer he was. He said,

"Spared, I spared them."

I turned, picked up the *dúidín,* and alarm lit his face. He shouted,

"Be careful, you imbecile, that's priceless!"

I snapped the stem, let the pieces fall, asked,

"And the fucking with me, the wreath, the mass card?"

He was staring at the ruined pieces, his eyes wet, said,

"An error of judgement, a momentary lapse of concentration, a frivolity that is alien to me; plus, I'd been tippling, a little too much of the Glenlivet. I apologise but then I felt you might be a worthy opponent."

My shout startled him.

"Opponent! You sick fuck, this isn't a game!"

He reached for his glass, sipped, then lit the pipe and composed himself, asked,

"What do you know about my wife?"

"What?"

"Ah, Jack, you'd make a poor student. Preparation, research, these are the keys."

The aroma of Clan filled the room, pungent, sweet, near cloying. I said,

"I found you."

"*Touché.* My wife had an inoperable tumour, suffered outrageous pain, then after years of anguish, when I wasn't home, she fell over some books I'd left at the top of the stairs."

I interjected,

"Books by Synge?"

He dismissed my interruption, continued,

"She was so peaceful there, curled at the bottom of the stairs. My beloved Deirdre."

Again I was thrown for a loop, went,

"That was her name?"

"Of course."

I refused to allow any sympathy to form, walked to the desk, picked up the third photo, asked,

"How did you get this?"

He smiled like he was definitely talking to an idiot, said,

"I'm a professor, I got it from college records; you think I don't have access to all areas?"

He smiled as if blessed.

"There was a woman went to bed at the lower village a while ago, and her child came along with her. For a time they did not sleep, and then something came to the window, and they heard a voice and this is what it said:
'It is time to sleep from this out.'
In the morning the child was dead, and indeed it is many get their death that way on the island."

J.M. Synge, *The Aran Islands*

I slammed the photo down on the desk, asked,

"Do you seriously think I'm going to let that happen? You're finished, pal."

His pipe had gone out and he tapped the bowl against an ashtray, a clay one with the faded letters:

Inishman

He sighed, said,

"Part of my plan was to engage someone's interest, and I was more than pleased that fate selected you. I hoped you might come to appreciate Synge; few do."

I sat, faced him, said,

"Sorry. The deaths of two girls obscured my appreciation of literature, and you know what? Synge is a pain in the ass."

He stood up, enraged, roared,

"You philistine! Synge didn't develop until late and yet was dead before his thirty-eighth year. Six short years of real creativity, yet he left a body of work without parallel."

I got as much scorn into my voice as I could, said,

"And you, you created two bodies, two grieving families, and you're plotting a third?"

He didn't reply, had shut me out. I said,

"I'm bringing you down, pal."

His head jerked and a tiny smile began to jig along his lips. He said,

"I think not. Superintendent Clancy and others of influence will crush your wild theories."

I reached over fast, slapped his head with the palm of my hand, said,

"You're not paying attention, Prof. I want to tell you about the Pikemen."

The slap had amazed him and he glared at me, said,

"Urban paranoia, if you mean the so-called vigilantes."

I spoke slowly, told him about Pat Young, the castration, then added,

"They've asked me to join them. Imagine that. So I'm going to bring your green file and your activities to them. You can be my first recommendation."

The blood had left his face and I said,

"This desk, yeah, they could hold you here. I think they'll have to use a gag, as slicing off your balls with a pike—I got to tell you, it's messy. I can't guarantee the instrument is even all that sharp. But tell you what, I'll ask them to put a copy of a book by Synge under you. An appropriate gesture, don't you think? Almost literary."

I put the file under my arm, walked past him, stopped at the door, said,

"But there is an alternative; you'll see it in the garage. It's a touch melodramatic I grant you, but, hey, you're the Dramatist."

Literary Ireland turned up en masse for the professor's funeral.
All the tired usual suspects who hadn't acknowledged him
in years lauded the two books on drama he'd written. That
these volumes had been out of print for years wasn't mentioned. The papers gave him polite obituaries, and one ar-
ticle hinted at his death as a tragic accident. Between the
lines was the unspoken word, managing to convey the sad
accidental deaths of his wife and brother, the strain of suicide never actually articulated.

I was in Nestor's, reading all this, a cup of neglected coffee before me. Jeff was changing a barrel and we were
dancing around the chasm between us. The sentry was
watching Sky News, the battle for Baghdad at its height.
Man U had walloped Liverpool by four goals. Leeds, despite their troubles, put six past Bolton. Ferguson was sug-
gesting that Man U's draw against Real Madrid was a fix.

The weather was glorious, probably our summer, though

May was a while away yet. Margaret had called to say she wouldn't see me for a time till I got my priorities straight. I'd said,

"Fine."

Cathy appeared, asked,

"Jack, would you sit with Serena May for an hour?"

"Sure."

I went upstairs and the little girl was delighted to see me, gave me one of those warm hugs. She was more energetic than usual, scooting around the room, gurgling happily. I felt bone weary but read for a bit to her, though neither of us was riveted. I opened the window to ease the heat, looked down on Forster Street, jammed with people. I went back, sat at the table, said to Serena,

"Hon, I'm going to buy you some new books tomorrow, how would that be?"

She gave the thumbs up. The first time I'd shown her, she was intrigued, and it had become a regular gesture with us now.

I thought about the professor and realised I'd become a Pikeman. The very act of vigilantism that put distance between Jeff and me was the same as what I'd done to the Dramatist. I hadn't yet contacted Stewart, wondered if I should make the trip to Mountjoy. I don't know how long I was sunk in those thoughts, probably only minutes, when I heard a small alarmed scream, then a chorus of horror rise up from the street.

I turned, the window was wide open. Serena May was gone.

*I don't know the name of this pub. It's new and some sort of aw-*ful techno is on the speakers. I've got a corner table and there's a full glass of Jameson near my right hand, within spitting distance so to speak. An untouched pint of Guinness is shadowing it, standing point. I was in Garavan's, was it yesterday? And when I came out, a group of school kids were messing on the street. One of them shouted "Hey, Johnny the limp!" I looked back and I swear one of them was the twin of Niall O'Shea, who leaped from the crane. I'm not too sure how long I was in Garavan's, but I heard a man mention the sadness of the small white coffin and I had to get out.

The day before, I bought sixty Major in Holland's. Mary spoke to me, but her words didn't seem to make sense. In the shop beside the canal, I got a shiny new lighter. I like it as it has the Galway crest on the side. I've put them to the very left of the drinks. It seems important the table look neat, everything in its place. Symmetry, is that the word?

If I ever go back to Bailey's, I might look it up, check the spelling.